Fami

presents

PATTI PINKERTON MYSTERY STORIES™

Book One

Trouble at The Cave

Carla Tedrow

FamilyVision Press, Inc.

New York

FamilyVision Press™

For The Family That Reads Together™

An imprint of Multi Media Communicators, Inc.
575 Madison Avenue, Suite 1006
New York, NY 10022

Managing Editor, Maggie Holmes
Typesetter, Samuel Chapin

Library of Congress Catalog Card Number: 93-71558

ISBN 1-56969-175-4

10 9 8 7 6 5 4 3 2

Printed in the United States of America

Girls *Can* Do It!

For all the girls who watched
Home Alone and said, "I could do that."

Well, you can.

TABLE OF CONTENTS

Trouble at The Cave

CHAPTER 1

It's Hard To Be Thirteen

It's hard to be thirteen and have a police-woman for a sister and a monster for a little brother. I've also got a fat, lazy dog named Susie Q and a cat named Pretty Girl which bites everyone but my dad.

But that's the story of my life. That's the story of Patti Pinkerton, would-be girl detective.

Everyone calls me Pink but lately I've been kind of blue. I want to be a detective. Not a real one. I'm too young. But I want to practice being one until I'm grown up.

I wish my dad was a detective, or my mom, then they could show me the ropes on Take Our Daughters to Work Days. But they're not. Dad works for the city, my mom's a secretary. I want to be a detective: Patti Pinkerton, Girl Detective.

But no one wants to give me a chance. Just because I'm only in seventh grade, always dress in pink, and can't see over the steering wheel, much less drive a car, doesn't mean I can't be a detective.

You see, I'm related to a famous one. One of the best. Allan Pinkerton, America's first detective, is my great-great-, maybe even great-great-great-, grandfather. He set up the Pinkerton Detective Agency in Chicago and opened branches all over America.

He set up a spy network for President Lincoln and worked on many famous cases. Yup, that's what my greater-than-great-granddad did.

But that was over a hundred and forty years ago. In Chicago. And he was a great man and I'm only a thirteen-year old kid who lives in Winter Park, Florida.

Winter Park is just a stone's throw from Orlando, the home of Mickey Mouse. It's great if you're a kid and want to go to Fantasyland, but when you get older like me, you're supposed to act cool.

Of course I secretly think going to Disney World is pretty neat, but it's not cool with my friends. So when I want to be cool, I go to the 7-Eleven where my friends hang out.

Enough of that. Like I was saying, all I want is to be a detective. Just snoop around and learn the ropes. Just like Grandpa, the great Pinkerton did.

But no one wants to give me a chance. It's hard to be thirteen.

CHAPTER 2

My Attic Domain

Hold on. Something's being slid under my attic door. Ugh! Just another stupid note from my dumb brother.

That's why I keep the attic door locked. The third floor is my domain. My place. I value my privacy. Everyone's supposed to knock when they come up here. My mother thinks it's puberty. My dad thinks it's kind of squirrelly. My friends think it's wild.

But the truth is, I keep the door locked to keep my monster brother, Wily the redhead, out of the attic. He likes to come up and mess with my Macintosh computer.

I made the mistake of showing him all the gadgets I'd rigged up to the computer—modems, phone data banks, a fax machine—used gadgets that I'd bought with the babysitting money I'd saved.

He thought it was cool and wanted to be a detective too. Said we could call ourselves, "Pinkerton and Pinkerton," I said *no way*.

It would be more like "Pinkerton and Little Rat," or "Pinkerton and Freckles the Monster."

He didn't laugh and threatened to tell Mom and Dad about the gadgets in the attic. And he's been trying to blackmail me ever since.

Not that I wasn't supposed to have them. That's okay. He was going to tell the folks what I was using them for...

DETECTIVE WORK.

You see, I got the Mac on my twelfth birthday so I could do my homework better. I'd clipped all the articles in *Scholastic* about how computers can help raise your grades. How they can open up a whole new world. Make you "yearn for education."

Yearn for education. That's the article that really got to Dad. Made him think of the old school days, back in the dark ages, when he went to school. Back before they had VCRs.

Sometimes he makes it sound like the days of President Lincoln, back when my great-great-grandpa was making his moves as a detective.

So they got me the computer and I hooked it up to all kinds of stuff. Stuff that opens all kinds of things. Like files in places where you're not supposed to look.

But that's what a good detective is supposed to do: get into places and ferret out facts. Just like a good student. That's why I didn't think it was a fib to let them think I needed the Mac for education.

Heck, I wanted to learn to be a detective. That's education, isn't it?

Geesh, will you look at this? My brother sent me another one of his stupid notes.

Let me in or I'll tell on you.

"Did you read it?" Wily giggled from the other side of the locked attic door.

"Yeah. It's stupid, just like you."

"Can I come in?"

"What's the password?" I asked. I change the password every day so he's never allowed in.

"'Pinkerton,'" he said.

"No. Now go away."

"Is it, 'pretty please'?" he asked.

"No, and will you 'pretty please' split out of here. Monster boys are not allowed in."

"Is the password 'Get Downstairs 'cause Dad's mad as heck'?"

I stopped. "What did you say?"

"Open the door and I'll tell you."

"No," I said. It was probably just a trick.

But my brother sounded too sure of himself, too cool to be bluffing. "Open the door. You're in trouble. The police are downstairs."

"Police?" I exclaimed, opening the door.

There stood my smiling little redheaded, freckled faced, part imp, all monster brother. He was nodding. Like the cat who swallowed the canary.

"Yup. The police are downstairs. Randy's in trouble again."

CHAPTER 3

Gator Trouble

Randy was the name of my alligator. Well, not mine really. He lives in the lake behind the house.

Randy hangs around near our pool. We don't feed him or anything like that, 'cause that's against the law. He just sort of fell in love with the stone alligator statue that we bought at a stupid flea market.

Dad said the gator was a randy teenager on the prowl. I wasn't sure what that meant, so I nicknamed him Randy, which seemed to make Mom and Dad laugh. The name stuck.

My mom was glad that someone actually liked the ugly cement gator.

I had to admit, the statue was ugly. I mean U-G-L-Y, ugly. Like Baby Herman in *Roger Rabbit.*

No one except Mom liked it, so we moved it from the front yard to the backyard. Way back near the edge of the lake. And that's where we first met Randy, the alligator who fell in love with our cement statue.

The problem is that while Randy doesn't bother us, he *does* freak out the neighbors. Like trying to eat their dogs or swimming in their pools.

Or like last Sunday, when the Greenbergs were having some bigwig party at their house. Randy just wanted to check it out, so he crept under the food table when they were all in the front yard.

You can't blame a gator for getting hungry and all that meat was just laying there. He ate about ninety steaks and then started biting into soda and beer cans. Guess he was thirsty.

It would have been okay if it had just been the sodas, but my dad said something about Randy ruining the beer and other things. Then he crawled into the Greenbergs' house and got kind of lost and messed up the place.

Randy gator-slimed their rugs and did the crocodile on their bed. The Greenbergs got really mad.

* * *

"Are you zoning out on me?" Wily asked.

I stopped daydreaming. "What did Randy do this time?" I asked my brother.

"Mrs. Crown says he tried to eat her little dog."

"Did he?"

Wily shrugged. "I guess Randy thought it was a snack or something. You know how Randy is," Wily said.

An understatement. Randy was *always* hungry. And dogs must look pretty good to a hungry gator.

Anyway, where was I? Oh yes, Wily said the police were downstairs.

"How many policemen are here?" I asked.

Wily closed his eyes. "Ah, ah, well actually..."

I hated the way he always beat around the bush. "Just exactly how many cops are down there?"

"Only one."

"One? I thought you said police plural."

"I did," Wily said, "but I made a mistake."

"Does Carol know that a policeman is here?" It was nice having a policewoman sister because she could help get you out of jams. Like Randy jams.

Wily nodded. "Carol knows."

"Did you call her?" I asked. Wily shook his head. "Did Dad call her?" Wily again shook his head no.

I was getting frustrated. "Did Mom call her?"

"No," Wily exclaimed, "don't you understand?"

"No, I don't understand," I said.

Wily put on his worst mischievous face. "I'll tell you if you let me know the password for getting into your room."

That was that. Nothing he knew or could say was worth having him know the password to enter my hideaway.

"Crawl back into your hole," I said.

"Pink, if I guess it will you let me in?"

"That's what a password's for." I nodded, not wanting to admit that there wasn't a snowball's chance of his guessing it.

And I'll tell you a secret. Even if he did, I'd probably get temporary amnesia and make up another word.

"Want to hear my ten reasons why Patti shouldn't be a detective."

"You've been watching Letterman too much." He wasn't supposed to stay up that late, but with the earphones and the TV set on the nightstand by his bed, it was no wonder he had gotten away with it and no wonder he had hound-dog bags under his eyes at the breakfast table.

"No, I haven't," he said, crossing his arms.

"Then where did you get the idea for ten of anything?"

Wily thought for a moment. His name was really William, but I nicknamed him Wily years ago. Like Wile E. Coyote. He is persistently annoying.

"Well," he began, "I was singing the 'Ten Little Indians' song and..."

"And you can stop right there," I said. "All I really want to know is how Carol knows about the policeman downstairs?"

"It's not a policeman."

"Okay, how does Carol know about the policewoman downstairs?" I asked, now wanting to tie him up, paint him green and stake him down on the ground next to the cement alligator.

"Carol knows 'cause she's downstairs."

"Why didn't you say so!" I shouted.

"That's what I was trying to tell you!" he called after me.

CHAPTER 4

Cop Sister

Having a cop for a sister is pretty neat. You get to ride in a squad car, go down to the station and watch them book the bad guys.

I've been asking her to take me on a night ride, but she says that their insurance won't allow for it.

That's really a drag. I mean, how can a thirteen-year-old would-be detective learn the ropes if some insurance company blocks your way?

But all that wasn't really on my mind as I came down the stairs as quickly as I could. I spun around the second floor rail and practically jumped the last flight down to the foyer.

Why they don't call it a waiting room like they do at the doctor's office, I'll never know. Foyer. Foy-er? Foy-ay?

"Hey, Patti, how you been, kid?" my policewoman sister Carol asked with arms open wide.

"I jumped into her arms. Can I ride in the patrol car with you, Sis?" I liked to call her Sis.

Carol shook her head. "Can't today. I'm doing public relations work at the mall."

My father coughed. "I don't know what we're going to do about that gator."

"You're lucky *I* caught the call. Mrs. Crown is fit to be tied," Carol said.

"But Randy didn't eat her stupid dog, did he?" I asked, suddenly feeling like Patti Pinkerton, defender of all things big and small.

Carol shook her head. "I told you that I can't keep the state Fish and Game Commission from coming here if Randy does eat a dog."

My father Al Pinkerton came in through the front door. Pretty Girl the cat was weaving between his legs, hoping for a treat.

"I think I've gotten her calmed down."

Talking to the grumpy neighbor must have upset my Dad because he kept on complaining. "It was worse than listening to rap music, I mean, you'd have thought that Randy was a murderer."

My mother came in right behind my father.

"Honestly, Patti, that Randy has got to go," Mom said. "If looks could kill, your father and I would both be dead. You wouldn't believe how that woman looked at us."

"You should have heard her call to the station," Carol laughed.

"I should have worn my animal-rights button over there," my father laughed. He sometimes wore a button that said, *I love animals...They're delicious.*

Mom was clearly upset. She got nervous about most things, but now she was really upset. "It was bad enough that your gator messed up the Greenbergs' house."

"Randy was just sleepy," I said, trying to be a defender of the environment.

"He was gator drunk," my father said.

Wily snickered from the stairs.

"William!" my mother said, as if by addressing him with his birth-certificate name would change him from a monster to something respectable.

"It's true!" Wily said, jumping down the last three stairs.

"How you doin', sport?" Carol asked.

"Shot anybody yet?" Wily asked, holding his fingers like a gun.

"William, you go to your room!" my mother said indignantly.

My brother just stood there as he always did, waiting for the final scream. It's funny how kids know to do that. Wait until the boiling point.

Carol patted Wily on the back. "You got any ideas on what we should do about Randy?"

"Take him to the vet and get him fixed," Wily said.

"William!" my mother gasped.

I thought she was going to have a fit. My brother was too mature for his own good. But Mom didn't watch MTV so she didn't know how mature some kids were.

Carol stood back and looked at me. "You're looking good, Pink," she said.

"Thanks, Sis," I nodded, wanting to blush. But my brother was looking at me.

"Liar, liar, pants on fire," Wily said, jabbing me with his elbow. "Pink's not pretty."

"Wily, go to your room," my father said.

Wily didn't move.

"William, go to your room," my mother said.

"All right," he said, slinking off.

"And don't play Nintendo," my father added. "Read a book for a change." He looked at me. "I can't understand why Wily wanted to hurt your feelings, Pink. You're a pretty girl. Don't let it get you down."

"Wily didn't mean that," Carol said, trying to lift my spirits.

I must have looked upset, but it wasn't from Wily's comment. Heck, I'm pretty. I've even been whistled at.

No, I was just feeling down, thinking about poor Randy, the lonely gator. "Is Mrs. Crown going to call the Fish and Game?"

"I told her I'd handle things," Carol said, reaching into her pocket.

"Then you should call Fish and Game," my mother replied.

"No, Mom," Carol said, shaking her head.

"Why not?"

"Because they'd just come over here and take Randy away. I've got a better idea," Carol smiled.

"Like what?" I asked.

"Like this," Carol said, handing me a cassette tape.

"What's that?" I asked.

Carol winked at Dad. "I asked a friend down at the Orlando Science Center to make a tape of gator mating calls."

"What for?" my mother asked.

"To trick Randy," my father surmised.

Carol nodded. "When Randy goes out on the prowl just pop this into Wily's boom box and lead him back to the lake. He'll think he's following a girl gator."

My dad laughed. "Think it will work?"

Carol nodded. "Just don't play it too loud or you'll have every gator in the lake dancing up into the yard."

"And then Mrs. Crown would really freak," I giggled.

"She loves that little dog," my mother said, shaking her head.

"Yeah," my father agreed.

I looked at Dad. He knew that I knew that he always whispered that he wished the little yapping dog would drown in the lake. A gator bite would be just as good.

Mrs. Crown's pet was a yapper. Yap, yap, yap, all night long. Just like she did when she came over to complain about Randy. Yap, yap, yap.

The dog's name was Sir Winston. I called him *Footlong,* Randy probably called him *Little Appetizer.* Dad, I can't even imagine what he called the dog.

In any event, losing him would be a loss only to Mrs. Crown. All of us, though we might not admit it, would be glad to see him disappear.

Suddenly, I was jarred out of my day-dreaming by a crackling, muzzy sound.

Sis's police radio went off.

CHAPTER 5

First Case

"Someone's calling you," Mom said, as if she were the only person in the world who heard the loud squawk.

"Thanks, Mom," Carol said.

The portable radio on Sis's belt was babbling. A voice was shouting something in police garble about a problem at a place called The Cave.

"Again?" Sue said into the mike.

She switched off the radio and looked at my father. "There's got to be a way to close down The Cave," she frowned.

My ears perked up. The Cave. That was a biker bar in a no-man's land between Winter Park and Orlando.

It was a place that people whispered about and drove blocks to avoid. A place where tough bikers hung out. A place where all kinds of things happen that a thirteen-year-old kid is not supposed to know about.

But I watch *Hard Copy* and *Inside Edition* and read the tabloids, so I know what goes on in the world. I'm not naive you know. I *am* thirteen.

"More trouble down there?" my father asked. Pretty Girl the cat clung to my Dad's ankles as if he was velcro.

My sister nodded. "That place is bad news. We've been trying to bust them for a year now, but we can't get a handle on them."

"Them?" my mother asked.

"The owners, the crooks who control the place," my sister sighed.

"Can't you just pull their liquor license?" my father asked.

My sister shook her head. "I wish it were that easy. We know the creeps in there are pushing dope and planning crimes, but we can't do anything without proof. We can't even go in there without being hassled."

"But you're the police," my mother said, as if the badge on my sister's uniform was stronger than kryptonite.

"Unless we get a violation we can hang on them, we can't close them down." Then my sister grinned. "'Course, if we could prove the place is owned by criminals, then we could shut it down."

That's when I grinned. I didn't say anything, but I grinned. Me, Patti Pinkerton. Pink. The thirteen-year-old great-great-granddaughter of America's greatest detective would shut them down. A detective who's been looking for a case to solve had finally found one.

Upstairs I had a computer that was just waiting to solve a crime. A crime that my sister had just handed to me on a silver platter. So I turned to go up the stairs.

"Where are you going?" my father asked.

I shrugged. "I have some work to do," I said, taking the stairs two at a time.

My sister laughed. "Teenagers, what do you expect?"

I grinned. Expect me to solve the case. But my happy thoughts were soon broken by the voice of a rat. Brother rat.

"What's the password?" Wily whispered.

"Stay in your room and you'll live to be ten."

"I'll tell Dad that you're not using your computer for homework," Wily smirked.

"That's blackmail."

"I know it," Wily grinned. "Now what's the password?"

"I'll tell you what," I said, pinching his arm. "I'll give you a free pass for the day, but I won't tell you the password."

"Okay, let's do it!" he exclaimed, pumping his fist in the air like he was some big macho football player. "Pinkerton and Pinkerton, together at last."

"Let's do what?" I asked, stopping him.

"Solve the case," Wily said.

"Solve what case?"

"The Cave," he grinned. "I heard what Sis said and..."

I was saved by my father's interruption. "Wily, get back in your room and leave your sister alone."

"Yes, Dad," he said.

"See ya," I said smugly, heading up to the attic.

I turned the key to the attic door and entered my office. *My office.* Sounds pretty important for a teenager.

I was ready. Thirteen-year-old Patti Pinkerton, detective, private eye, was ready to start her very first case.

Not bad for a kid who didn't even have a driver's license.

CHAPTER 6
Password

I stood in the center of my room looking at the musty old portrait of great-great-grandfather Allan Pinkerton. My kind of guy.

Got a job when he was twelve. Had to skip out of Scotland because the police were after him in 1842. He wasn't a crook or anything—he had been demonstrating for his rights.

He got married as he boarded the ship and headed to Chicago. Soon he traced down and turned in some counterfeiters and was made a deputy sheriff. From there he became Chicago's first private detective.

He teamed up with a lawyer named Rucker and they opened a detective agency, which my ancestor expanded across the country. From there he set up a spy service for the Union, saved President Lincoln's life and then got his name all shot to blazes by the historians because he worked with the railroad owners against the unions.

I looked at the portrait of the old great one and asked, "How did *you* handle your first case?"

Then I really looked at the eyes. Though he'd been dead over a hundred years, I thought I could feel his presence in the room.

Then I felt another presence. It was my freckle-faced midget of a brother.

"Get out!" I snapped.

"Do you want to hear my ten reasons why you won't make a good detective?"

"I'll give you one good reason to split," I said, making a fist.

"You left the door open," Wily grinned like he'd just won an Oscar for smarts.

"Thanks for telling me," I said, pushing him toward the door.

"What are you doing?"

"I'm pushing you out. Then I'm going to close the door and lock you out once and for all."

"But I came up to ask you a question," he said, holding out a book.

"What's the question?" I asked wearily.

"What's the password?"

"No way," I said, turning back towards the attic door. I waited for him to leave. "Good-bye, adios, split."

Still no footsteps. "Go change your shirt or something," I said without turning around. I waited some more but the silence was killing me. Finally I turned. "Get out of here."

"I'll be good."

"Will you be quiet? Like lips zipped?" Wily nodded. "Okay, then you can stay for a few minutes."

I went about my business getting ready for my first case. I sharpened a pencil, wrote my name on a piece of paper, broke the pencil lead, sharpened the pencil again. . . just the things that a detective has to do to begin.

I switched on the computer, opened the phone data lines and was ready to begin. But I wasn't sure exactly what to do first.

"Changed your security code didn't you?" Wily said quietly from behind.

"How'd you know that?" I asked. Yes, I had changed my code, but I hadn't told anyone. Just my diary.

Then it hit me. *Just my diary!*

"I told you to never read my diary," I said, my eyes flaring.

Wily is the only kid in the world who can moonwalk with his mouth. "It was open when I was walking by and I thought someone had lost it and..."

"And you snooped," I frowned.

"I was just practicing to be a detective," he shrugged. "Like you."

I turned back to the computer and punched in a city map. Using a few tricks of the detective trade, I located The Cave, and then entered the city's information data base to find what name was on the business license.

"Where'd you learn to do that?" Wily whispered in awe.

I guess it *was* pretty impressive. Here I was, a thirteen-year-old operating technology like a pro.

"I just read a lot, that's all," I said, flustered, not used to a real compliment from such a brat.

"That's why we'll make a good detective team," he said. "Pinkerton and Pinkerton. High tech and low tech."

I saved the material I was working on and looked at him. "High tech and low tech?"

Wily grinned. "Sure. You got the computer and I got the low tech stuff."

"Like what?" I said, not sure I wanted to know.

He unstrapped the nerd pack he always had hooked to his belt. "Low tech is stuff like this," he bragged. He pulled out a kid's arsenal. Stink bombs, itching powder, gas powder, smoke bombs—a regular PTA nightmare.

"Where'd you get all this?" I asked, hoping he wouldn't drop the stink bombs. I didn't want my pretty pink attic to smell like a million rotten eggs.

"It's all one hundred percent street legal."

"Aren't you supposed to be eighteen to buy this stuff?" I asked, looking at his *Home Alone* war arsenal.

Wily shrugged. "I bought it all through the mail."

"But what about the part where they ask if you're eighteen?"

Wily laughed. "Eighteen? I thought it asked if I was *eight*."

I let that one slide. Through the mail, he said. My brother was a regular mail-order terrorist.

"And what do you do with this?" I asked, picking up the gas powder packet.

Wily grinned. "You put this in someone's drink or food and it makes them pass gas like an elephant."

"No way!" I said, looking at the packet.

"It's true," Wily nodded.

"Have you ever tried it?"

Wily thought for a moment. "Promise not to tell?" I nodded. "Remember after the Greenberg's party when Dad heard all the noises."

I smiled. Dad had complained that he thought the neighbors were acting like kids. Mom thought they were just making "goosing sounds" under their arms as she politely called it.

"I remember," I said.

"Well," Wily snickered, raising his eyebrows, "I snuck over when the cops came and I put the gas powder into their punch bowl and..." he paused and looked at me.

"No!"

"Yes!" he laughed. "And it sounded like a tornado had broken loose."

I laughed so hard I cried. I couldn't help but believe my brother. I mean, here he was, an imp with an arsenal of stink bombs, smoke bombs, itching powder and gas powder, having tricked the neighbors. "You'd better never let Mom and Dad find out," I said between laughs.

I guess I would have been mad if they'd been nice neighbors, but the Greenbergs were so mean. Still I couldn't approve what he did. At least, not on the outside.

So I straightened up. "Don't let Dad find this stuff."

"He thinks I carry my allowance in it," Wily snickered again.

Dad shouted from downstairs, "Wily, come down here."

"Will you tell me the password?" Wily begged.

"No." I could be tough when I had to be.

"Please. I've got to go."

"No, it's a secret password. You've got to guess."

Wily turned to go, then spun around. "One day you're going to be in trouble and you'll need my help. I hope you'll know *my* password."

I started to say something but didn't. Sometimes you got to be tough on a kid. Helps them grow up. Become street smart, learn the ropes.

That's how I've survived for thirteen long years.

CHAPTER 7

Red Ribbon Friends

It wasn't five minutes after Wily left when my phone rang. Since it was my private line, I decided to answer it very business-like.

"Pinkerton Agency, whom would you like to speak to?" I asked in my best middle-aged voice.

There was a pause on the line, then the voice of my friend Sarah squeaked out, "Can I speak to Patti Pinkerton please?"

"One moment," I said, putting the phone on hold and bursting out laughing.

Sarah lived across the street. She must have seen my sister's squad car pull into the driveway, and being the noisy type, called to get the latest.

When I was calmed down, I pushed the button to get back on the line. "Patti here."

"Who was that answering the phone?" Sarah asked. "Your mom?"

"Do you think my mom would answer my phone for me?" I asked.

"Is your mom selling insurance no?"

"Selling insurance?"

"She said Pinkerton Agency. I'm totally, one hundred percent confused," Sarah moaned, wishing she hadn't called.

"No, the Pinkerton *Detective* Agency. I just opened my own private eye company. What do you think?"

"I think you're crazy and I'm going to hang up," Sarah said.

I started to give her a hard time but stopped. Life had given Sarah a hard enough time. That's why I wear a red ribbon on my shirt. Like I saw the stars at the Academy Awards wear.

You see, Sarah has AIDS. More than HIV positive. Full blown. She got it from a blood transfusion.

Sarah's a hemophiliac. Which means she needs lots of blood transfusions to stay alive.

The doctor says she now has AIDS-related pneumonia and tuberculosis. I can't even pronounce it but I know it's a drag. That's why she stays mostly in bed.

But she's a good kid and isn't down on life the way it is down on her. She was always wanting to know the neighborhood goings-on.

She stayed glued to her bedroom window. Which was why she knew what was happening in the neighborhood.

When she was having a bad day, all she could do was lay in her room and look outside. Her mom had propped up the bed so she could see the street. With the telescope she had, why she had her eyes on everything.

"What was the police car doing in your driveway, Pink?"

"That was my sister."

"Was she just coming for lunch or what?"

I had to give it to Sarah, she was very persistent. Like a bulldog.

"Mrs. Crown complained about Randy again."

"Did he finally eat her dog?" Sarah giggled, like it was the funniest thing she'd heard all day.

"No, but she had a double-cow and a stroke and was flipping out over it all."

Then Sarah sighed. "I guess soon they'll come take Randy away and make him into gator sandwiches or something."

"I hope not."

"You better get prepared for the day."

I didn't want to think about it so I changed the subject. "How're you feeling today?"

"Not too good, Pink." She paused. I just waited for her to catch her breath.

"Want me to tell you about how ignorant Wily's been acting again?"

Sarah didn't say anything. The last time I had her in stitches telling her about how Wily had gotten arrested for taking Dad's golf cart down to the 7-Eleven. The policeman didn't think it was funny when he showed him a Blockbuster Video card and said it was his driver's license.

But I told Sarah that on one of her good days. This one didn't sound so good for her so I just waited until she was strong enough to speak again.

"Tell me about the detective agency," she managed to whisper.

And so I began talking. It was a strange friendship that Sarah and I had. When she ran out of breath, I just turned on my mega-mouth and went into verbal overdrive.

Just talk, talk, talk. Always trying to be cheerful, telling Sarah everything I was doing.

It was like she was experiencing what she couldn't experience through me. Like she was with me doing the things I did.

I guess it was the red ribbon I wore for her. Maybe there's something psychic between us. ESP or something. Or maybe we're just good friends and we care for each other. You figure it out.

After I finished the hip-hop conversation I could tell Sarah needed to get off and rest. "Want me to hang up?" I asked.

"Are you wearing my ribbon?" she asked.

My ribbon. That's what she called the red ribbon. To stars they were AIDS Awareness Ribbons, but to Sarah, it was *my ribbon.*

She was the only person with AIDS that I knew and it made me really appreciate life. "Yup, I've got your ribbon on," I whispered, feeling my eyes well up.

"You're my red ribbon friend," she said, and then she hung up.

It wasn't like she was rude or anything, it was just that she was tired. And I understood because I was her friend, her red ribbon friend.

I might have cried for Sarah right there on the spot if I hadn't heard all the racket outside. Looking out, I couldn't believe what I saw.

CHAPTER 8

Hang Ten

At first I thought it was a kid with Bigfoot's skateboard, but then I realized it was our neighbor, Mr. Carpenter. He was seventy-two going on six. A funny old know-it-all who did whatever the heck he felt like.

Mr. Carpenter was speeding across his yard on a motorized scooter. Not just a scooter-scooter. This was an old surfboard on wheels with a motor on it, and man, was he ever flying!

Mr. Carpenter zoomed through the yard and just about dropped his false teeth when he bumped over the curb. "Polygrip works!" he shouted, throwing his fist in the air like he was a kid.

Then he did a wheelie, or whatever you call raising up the front wheels on a motorized surfboard. I smiled. You had to be there to see it.

Imagine if you had a seventy-two-year-old neighbor who just happened to come surfing across your yard on a motorized skate board.

What would you think? You'd probably think it was pretty wild—that's what I thought.

"Ride 'em cowboy!" the mailman shouted as he drove past in his mail jeep.

"Just deliver my mail and be quiet," Mr. Carpenter shouted as he surfed across the street, around a telephone pole, and back toward my house.

Then I saw them. Two old ladies with canes were walking along.

"Hey, toots," Mr. Carpenter said, surfing past them. "You want to boogie at my place?" He gave them each a wink.

"Act your age," one of them said.

"Watch me go!" Mr. Carpenter said as he surfed circles around them.

"Go home," the other woman said, trying to get past.

Who could get mad at an old man so cool that he made a thirteen-year-old feel old and square? I mean, he was doing things I'd never dreamed of or would dare to do.

Wily shouted out from his window below, "Hang ten, Mr. Carpenter!"

"Come on out here and ride," old Mr. Carpenter cackled. "This thing's a gas!"

"Be right out," Wily shouted back.

Mr. Carpenter scooter-surfed through the hedges and across Mrs. Crown's flower beds. She came running out screaming but he just aimed his contraption her way and drove her back into her house.

"Get off my property! I'm calling the police!" she screamed at him from inside her screened porch.

"Call the President, call the F.B.I., or call for a pizza. What do I care? I'm retired. I'll just say I'm old and addle-brained!" Mr. Carpenter yelled back.

"You are that, you old fool," she said, going inside.

Then he noticed me staring out my window. "Get out here, Pink, and ride this thing!"

So what was I to say except, "I'll be right out!"

CHAPTER 9

Surfboard Boogie

I took the stairs two at a time, knocking the pictures on the walls off balance.

When I got out to the front porch, my mom was out there wringing her hands. Dad was shaking his head, pointing toward the front. I looked over and saw why.

My muffin-headed brother Wily was riding on the back of the motorized surfboard, holding onto Mr. Carpenter like they were on a bobsled in the Olympics.

"Oh dear," my mother said. That was it. That was all she could say. *Oh dear.*

My dad now, he was something else. He shouted, "Ride 'em cowboy!"

"Come on, Pink, hop on!" Mr. Carpenter shouted as he saw me.

"No you don't, Patti," my mother said.

I hesitated. If I jumped on, she'd be angry. If I just watched, I'd be bored. Tough choice between being responsible and being a kid.

The kid won out. I jumped off the porch and ran alongside the surfboard on wheels. "Wait for me," I screamed and jumped on.

"This gizmo waits for no man..." Mr. Carpenter said, "...or woman." Wily held onto Mr. Carpenter's waist and stuck his tongue out at me.

"This thing is wild!" Wily shouted, for all the world to hear.

My mother cried out, "Get off that thing right this minute."

"Yes, Mother," Wily said. Then under his breath he whispered to Mr. Carpenter, "Let's go! Floor it!"

"Let's boogie!" Mr. Carpenter shouted.

On board, as if at the back of the conga line, I held onto freckle-head's waist.

"Don't tickle me," Wily said over the roar of the engine.

"Don't flatter yourself," I said, pinching what flab I could pull from his string-bean waist.

"Ouch!" Wily screamed, bending to his left.

"Watch it!" Mr. Carpenter shouted.

But it was too late. Wily had thrown the surfboard off course and we were headed for disaster. Up ahead, coming straight at us, was a telephone pole. To our left was a parked car and to our right was an old lady who'd come out from her house.

I was getting worried. Given the choice of hitting the telephone pole, a parked car, or an old lady, I pretty much knew what Mr. Carpenter's choice would be. But I had to say something, since I didn't want to be part of any lawsuit the old lady might file if we ran over her.

"Turn left," I yelled, figuring with luck we could avoid the parked car.

"No," Mr. Carpenter said, "we're going to hang a right."

Right toward the old lady. Her sourpuss face went from scowl to howl when she realized that we were going to run into her!

"You're gonna hit her!" I shouted.

"Maybe...maybe not." Mr. Carpenter said, gritting his teeth.

I couldn't tell if he was serious or not. That's the problem with old grown-ups. They learned their way of kidding before TV was invented, so it's kind of hard to know when they're pulling your leg.

But this old lady must have taken her vitamins, because as we plunged at her she did a sprint like she was trying out for the Olympics. "This is like playing Mario Cart," Wily laughed.

"Watch out!" I pleaded.

"Two points if you hit her," Wily grinned.

"You're on!" Mr. Carpenter laughed.

"Let me steer," Wily shouted, enjoying the old lady's dilemma.

"This is better than bowling," Mr. Carpenter screamed. But then the engine began to sputter. "Somebody up there likes her," he grumbled.

"You both come home right now," my mom demanded.

"Okay," I said.

We pushed the motorized skateboard back to his garage. "That was great," Mr. Carpenter smiled.

"Are you all right?" my mother shouted from our yard.

"Yeah, yeah, yeah," Wily said. "Geesh, can't she just leave me alone sometimes?"

"Mothers are like that," Mr. Carpenter grinned.

He got out a block of wax and began rubbing it on his surf board. "What are you doing?" Wily asked.

"Waxing down my board. What's it look like?"

"William Pinkerton, you come home right now," my mother screamed.

"Better git, boy," Mr. Carpenter said, tousling Wily's hair.

"That was fun," Wily said, reluctant to leave.

"Next time you take your Dad's golf cart and we'll race."

"You're on. Gotta go," Wily said, heading out of the garage.

CHAPTER 10

Clues

I was left alone with old Mr. Carpenter. All adults look old to kids and Mr. Carpenter was over seventy which made him seem ancient. Kind of like a living mummy.

Mr. Carpenter looked at me. "And you, Miss Patti "Pink" Pinkerton. What kind of trouble you been getting into?"

I shrugged. "Not much."

"Any boys kissed you yet?" he asked, giving me a big, big wink.

I shook my head. "Don't lie to me," he laughed. "Heck, I was a kid once and I ain't forgot the kisses I got from the girls when I was 'bout your age."

He had me dead to rights. A couple of boys *had* put their lips on my cheek and a cute guy named Robbie put his lips to mine when we were waiting in the lunch line. Even though someone had pushed him, his lips did hit mine, which counts for something, I guess.

I confessed. "Not really kissing," I blushed. "More like pecking," I said, hoping I had a word that he'd understand. After all, maybe they did it differently when he was a kid back in the dark ages.

Mr. Carpenter babbled on. "Make sure he's brushed his teeth." Then he laughed. "Just don't try kissin' anyone after they've eaten at a deli. Why I remember once kissin' this girl whose Pop owned a sandwich shop and, man, you can't believe how bad it is to kiss someone who tastes like salami."

"Gross," I said.

"Worse than gross," he laughed.

"Why'd you kiss her then?" I asked.

"Just curious. And speaking of curious, you found yourself a case yet?" he asked me.

"How did you know I was looking for one?"

"Wily told me. Said you were investigating," his voice went quiet, "The Cave." Mr. Carpenter shook his head in concern. "Be careful 'round that place. Bad sorts go there."

I nodded. "My sister says it should be shut down."

"Was that why your sister was here earlier in her black-and-white?"

"No. Mrs. Crown complained about Randy again."

Mr. Carpenter let out a good old-fashioned belly-laugh. "That old coot. Why she just doesn't lighten up I'll never know."

"She said that Randy was trying to eat her dog."

"I wish he *had* eaten that noisy thing," Mr. Carpenter said. "I've even thought of eatin' it myself if that was the only way to shut that thing up."

"Yeah, my dad complains about the little yapper, too."

"Patti, come home now," I could hear my mom shouting.

But Mr. Carpenter continued. "So what's the problem with The Cave?" he asked.

"Police can't figure out who owns it. My sister says the real owners are hidden away in lots of paperwork."

Mr. Carpenter guffawed. "Shoot, they should just come and ask me."

"Ask you?"

He nodded. "Place is owned by Jack Seagel."

I held my breath. Jack Seagel was known as a big-time crook, even by kids like me.

"How do you know that?" I asked.

"Heck," Mr. Carpenter grinned, like I was the dumbest dumb-bunny in the world, "I used to hang out there when they first opened it."

"You did?"

"Yup, and I rode a Harley with the best of 'em."

"*You* rode a *Harley*?" I was flabbergasted.

"For about ten years."

"How long ago?" I asked.

"Back in the fifties. When they first opened. That's how I know it's Jack Seagel who owns it. Hasn't changed hands. He and I used to ride together and pick up girls and make fools of ourselves."

The thought made me smile. Guess it's good for a kid to think about old folks acting young and silly.

"Patti, come home now," my mom yelled a second time.

"I better get going."

Mr. Carpenter sighed. "If you need any information on that old crook Seagel, you just check with me."

"I will."

"Yup," he nodded, "I was there when that place had but one little rinky-dink coin-operated pool table. That's when it was a *real* pool room."

Then he stared off toward a tool-covered wall, with a dreamy look like he was in church. "I can see it now, an old sign that used to hang over the door: Gambling, Profanity, and the Consumption of Alcoholic Beverages on Premises Will NOT Be Tolerated." He shook his head.

"You okay, Mr. Carpenter?" I asked.

He sighed. "Just thinkin' back on the old days, Pink."

"You mean like in old days at The Cave?"

"Yup. Back when there weren't no bar. Just a soft-drink machine so the old coots and punks could have something to mix with their hip-pocket bottles."

"Patti, come home *now*!" my mom yelled. That was the third time. It *was* time to leave.

"You've been a big help, Mr. Carpenter," I said, turning to go.

The phone rang. For some reason I waited. Mr. Carpenter took it from the kitchen wall which connected with the garage. He said hello, then looked at me.

"It's for you."

"For me?"

"Yup," he nodded, handing it to me.

"Hello?" I said hesitantly, figuring it was my mom going ballistic on me for not coming home.

I was wrong. It was Sarah. "Pink, you'd better get home. Your mom's flipping out."

"Thanks for calling," I said.

"Call me later. I want to hear all about what Mr. Carpenter's been telling you."

"Okay," I said, hanging up.

Mr. Carpenter smiled. "Come on back later and I'll tell you more about that ol' crook Jack Seagel."

"Why do you keep calling him a crook?" I asked.

"Because he still owes me the fifty bucks that I loaned him back in 'fifty-seven to open the place."

"You loaned him money to open The Cave?"

"Yup. Without my fifty, ol' Seagel would still be pumpin' gas at the Texaco station." He scratched his head. "Still got the IOU note 'round here someplace."

"I'd like to see that," I said, knowing that a good detective checks out all the clues.

"When I find it I'll call you," he said. Then he began looking into old drawers and boxes, like he was rummaging at a flea market. "I know that durn thing's round here someplace."

"Good luck. See ya," I said. But at the door I stopped. "Mr. Carpenter, what did you do with your old Harley?" I asked.

"Gertie?"

"Gertie?"

"Gertie, my hog."

Now, I was really confused. "You own a *hog*?"

"Not a farm hog, missy. I'm talking about Gertie, my Harley-Davidson motorized hog. Hog was a nickname for motorcycle."

"Well, what did you do with Gertie?" I asked.

"Nothing. It's over there," he smiled, pointing to a tarpaulin-covered object in the corner of the garage.

"Can I see it?"

"Certainly," he said, and walked over. He took the corner off the tarp, then hesitated, like he was about to uncover something from his past that he hadn't seen for awhile.

"Been a long time," he whispered. Then he whipped the cover off.

"Oh my gosh," I whispered.

There stood the biggest, meanest, baddest motorcycle I'd ever seen. A Harley. A real Harley-Davidson. A hog. The mother of all motorcycles.

"This is no toy Japanese bike," he nodded.

"Does it still work?" I asked.

"Harley's work forever," he said. Reaching into a locker behind the cycle, he pulled out a leather jacket and pants, and a helmet. "And this here's my leathers," he said, rubbing them as if they were alive.

I just stood there. This old man who I thought was just sort of a kook had been a biker in the fifties!

I stood in awe and felt like saluting this real golden oldie. But the only words that came to mind were, "That's cool."

"It sure was," he whispered. "They called me Ramrod."

"Ramrod?" I whispered, like I'd just been let in on a real secret.

"Ramrod," he repeated, holding the leather jacket like it was going to dance with him or something.

"Patti, I want you to come home now," my mother's shout interrupted us.

"Now you better get on home," he said, hanging the jacket back up in the locker.

"Patti!" my mother shouted again.

From the tone I knew that my mother was steaming. For a moment I thought of my mother, standing on the porch, waving for me to come home.

"Get home, girl, before you get in trouble."

"If you find that IOU, call me," I said.

"And you can call me...Ramrod," Mr. Carpenter said, like just saying the name took forty years off his life.

"Okay, Ramrod," I grinned.

He straightened up his back. I had to admit he did look a bit younger. Maybe even sixty-five.

I took off for my house. I waved to Sarah and then saw Mom, standing impatiently, waiting for my return. Wondering what I could possible have in common with crazy old Mr. Carpenter.

Mr. Carpenter. *Ramrod. Cool.* Neater than cool. It was wild. And I'd also gotten my first lead on the case and I hadn't really revved up the old Mac yet.

I guess Fred Flintstone would shout, "yabba-dabba-doo," but I just pumped my fist into the air and shouted, "All right!"

I had set out on a course to be a detective. Heck, I was already halfway there. Halfway to solving my first case!

CHAPTER 11

Pranks

Sometimes the best laid plans of mice and men go haywire, at least that's what Dad says. In my case, my plans had an egg laid on them.

You see, while I was feeling pretty good about myself, my high-fat, low-brain brother Wily was pranking on The Cave. And not just one prank, he was major pranking!

While Patti, the would-be detective, was thinking about how I would slyly snoop around The Cave using the information that Ramrod had given me, my brother, the none-too-subtle idiot, was making prank calls to the club.

Though I didn't get the whole picture until later, this is the gist of what happened. My brother, who'd been caught before making crank calls to his teachers at school, had taken the portable phone into his room.

He was supposed to be reading, but instead closed the door so he could wreck mayhem, cause major damage, and be a gigantic pain-in-the-you-know-what to the sleaze down at The Cave.

Of course I would have told him not to do it. A good detective never gives the suspect a chance to think something's up.

But my brother? That freckle-head twit decided to stick it in their faces.

Just picture guys with skull tattoos, standing around a stinky, smoky bar, drinking and cussing, suddenly getting a call like this:

"Hello, is this The Cave?" Wily asked.

"Yes," the muscle-bound bartender said.

"Can I speak to the caveman?"

"He's not here."

"Well, tell him Fred Flintstone called!" my brother shouted, shrieking with laughter as he hung up the phone.

Now, you know what little rats seven-year-olds are. Or is he eight? It's hard to tell how old he is because most of the time he acts three going on two.

Anyway, my brother spent about an hour harassing the lunk heads and crooks down at the place I was supposed to be investigating.

He sent six pizzas to the bar, an order of Chinese food, an ambulance and two police cars.

And that wasn't all. He also had a bakery deliver twenty-two cakes and a pet shop bring over two lovebirds. He even called a church to have an emergency soul-saving team sent over.

But did my brother stop while he was ahead? *What do you think?*

He must have worn his fingers out pawing through the yellow pages. He sent over a plumber, a locksmith, a computer repair man, a caterer, the Sears bug-spray team, a pool cleaner and to top it off, had two truckloads of fresher-than-fresh, stink-to-high-heaven cow manure dumped in their parking lot.

It stunk bad. I mean *really* bad. Worse than bad. And the piston-heads down at The Cave wanted to stomp whoever did it.

"They'll never know," my brother crowed.

But while Wily Coyote was chuckling, the bartender was dialing Mr. Jack Seagel to complain about the pranks. The guy Ramrod said owned the joint.

Mr. Seagel was no dummy and evidently had a few IOUs from the phone company. So within an hour he had something called Caller ID installed on The Cave phone. It lets the person being pranked see the number of who is pranking.

If my brother had just stopped, they would never have discovered our number. But my midget monster brother had to make just one last call.

"Hello, Cave?"

The bartender recognized his voice which wasn't any amazing feat since Wily the mad caller had already called a few dozen times. The third florist of the day had just delivered a COD flower arrangement and the boys at The Cave weren't happy.

"Could you hold a minute and I'll be right with you," the tattooed and ugly bartender asked. He pushed the Caller ID button and *presto* our home phone number magically appeared.

"Now, can I help you?" the bartender asked.

I can just picture my brother's face, smiling smug as a potato bug. "Is Fred there?"

"Fred who?" asked the bartender, playing along.

"Flintstone. You know, the caveman," Wily said.

"Get this, you punk," the bartender whispered. "We know who you are and here's your number."

My brother dropped the phone as if it were a hot potato.

They knew the phone number. They'd be calling back.

CHAPTER 12

Super Snooper

While all this was going on, I was at home, quietly snooping on the computer, checking into data bank information about restaurants, bars, licenses and a bunch of stuff I didn't understand. To date, being a detective wasn't all that much fun. I mean, I thought I'd get a chance to wear a lot of disguises, not do all this math-type stuff.

But still, if that's what it took to be a detective, I was willing to do my time. And you wouldn't believe all the good stuff I found.

I decided to check on the name Jack Seagel in the city's business license section. I was not supposed to be doing that but I had the access codes. I, uh...borrowed them from my sister's procedures book. Not that I was supposed to have the access codes. My sister would have freaked out if she'd known I'd copied them.

I had them. So I used them. But this was what flashed up each time I entered a file that I wasn't supposed to:

Unauthorized Entry Into This System Is Punishable by Fine and Prison Term

The first time I saw it I panicked. But then I learned to close my eyes each time it came on. Sort of like what I didn't know wouldn't hurt me. Except that I did know, which is why I still don't understand why I closed my eyes.

Once inside the city's computer system, I found out a bunch about Mr. Jack Seagel. He owned a lot of things, but he didn't appear to own The Cave.

Why a multi-millionaire would want to own a sleazy place like The Cave was beyond me.

But then I remembered how I still saved things from when I was little and I made my first detective guess. "I bet he doesn't want to let go of the first place he ever owned!"

It made sense. Kids save things from the past for no reason, goofy things like bottle caps and broken keys, so why couldn't an adult do the same thing?

I was about to put a lot more thought into it when Sarah called and asked me to come over. Said she needed to talk. That she was feeling kind of down.

I switched off my computer and made for her house. Sure, I could have made up an excuse. I mean, no one likes to sit around the bed of someone who's sick.

But my Mom always taught me to be kind and considerate to others, so maybe this was my way of practicing what she preached.

Why should I make excuses? Sarah was my friend and I knew that one day, I'd come home and find out that she'd died. Which made me sad.

She'd never go on a first date. Never fall in love. She'd never go to the prom.

Heck, she might not live until the prom. So that's why I went. To kind of make peace with God for not always appreciating my life. Every time I saw Sarah I said a prayer, which was kind of weird, because so many kids think it's uncool to pray.

But talking to God makes you feel good. Or at least it did me. And besides, if you yakkity-yak to God, you find that He talks back if you give Him the chance. Which is pretty neat if you ask me.

So that's why I went over to see Sarah.

Later I found out that at almost that exact nanosecond, Ramrod was sitting in his garage, looking at the IOU for fifty bucks that Jack Seagel had given him, backed up by fifty percent ownership in The Cave if the note wasn't paid back in time.

Ramrod had also found a picture of himself and Seagel together, dressed in leathers and sitting on their Harleys. A picture over forty years old.

I also didn't know that my sister had pulled up the rap sheet on the bartenders and other employees of The Cave. If you don't know what a rap sheet is, think of it as a teacher's behavior report, only on adults.

I can picture her now, whistling, shaking her head as she read their list of crimes: Breaking and Entering, Grand Theft, Burglary, Shoplifting, Auto Theft, Assault.

At this point, I didn't knew how bad these guys were. I didn't know any of this at the time. I was happily cruising over to Sarah's. I didn't know that all heck was about to break loose.

CHAPTER 13

Sarah Talk

"Hey, Patti," Dad called out from his easy chair in the living room.

I stopped and turned. From the tone of his voice I knew he wanted something. If he was going to order me to do something, it was just, "Patti." If he was mad, it was "young lady" or "come here."

But "Hey, Patti," in a nice sing-song voice meant he wanted something. So my antenna was up.

"Yes, Dad?" I asked, putting on my thirteen-year-old going on two voice. I hoped my tone would sound babyish, like I was too young for whatever he wanted me to do.

"Would you do me a favor tonight and baby-sit your brother? Your mom and I are going out to dinner."

I caught my breath. Baby-sit Wily? That was like being asked to go into a lion's cage with a raw steak in your mouth.

I mean, come on! No one wants to baby-sit their brother. It's okay to baby-sit someone else's brats because you get paid and when the people are away, you get to blab on their phone and eat their junk food.

But baby-sit for your brother? No way. You don't get paid, you don't get any real appreciation, and you can't beat the tar out of the little dip when he acts up.

"Did you hear me, Patti?" my dad asked.

It was a no-win situation that I wanted no part of, so I said, "I've got a lot of homework to do."

"But you told me earlier that you already finished it."

I could feel the steel jaws of the truth trap coming down on me. My own words were being used to hang me!

"But I need to do some extra studying."

My dad nodded the nod that dads do when they know their kid is trying to weasel out of something. "I see. So we'll just let Wily watch the tube and you study."

"But TV's bad for kids, isn't that what you said?" I was trying to turn the tables and use his words back on him.

My dad was quick on his feet. He picked up the newspaper and scanned the TV section. "There's a nature show on. Let him watch that while you study."

Nature show. They were going out to dinner and I was going to have to *live* a nature show, baby-sitting a rabid wild rat-brat.

"Why don't you take Wily with you?" I suggested.

You should have seen my dad's face. He hated taking Wily out to dinner because no matter how hard they worked on the kid's table manners, he always acted like an animal.

I mean, he picked up food with his fingers, held the fork upside down, coughed, wiped his fingers on his pants and burped at the waiters.

In other words, Wily wasn't exactly the kind of kid you wanted to take out in public. He was definitely the kind you took through the drive-in of a fast-food place.

"Not tonight," my dad said.

No matter how I tried to talk my way out of it, I was stuck. "Okay, but he's got to take his own bath before you go."

I mean, no self-respecting thirteen-year-old would-be detective wants to have to run her brother's bath!

"No problem," Dad grinned. Strike three and I was out.

So I walked to Sarah's house like I was walking the plank. I straightened up my act by the time I got to her room because comparing my life to Sarah's, I had nothing to be down about.

Each time I walked up to Sarah's second-floor room, I felt sad.

My dad has a saying that he uses when he sees a person less fortunate. "There but for the grace of God go I." It came to me each time I approached her room.

No matter how you cut it, Sarah didn't ask for the HIV virus. AIDS came to her through the blood supply. You might blame the government, blame the Red Cross, heck blame the world, but no one can change the fact that my friend is sick and dying.

Even the new AZT drug they'd been giving her didn't seem to do much good. Her mom said that my visits did more good than all the drugs and pills in the world, which put a big load of responsibility on my shoulders.

So I rapped with Sarah, telling her about Ramrod, what I found on the computer, and the fact that I was going to have to baby-sit for the monster.

Sarah just listened, wheezing slightly. It wasn't a good day for her, but she did her best to laugh at the punch lines.

"And he really for real called himself Ramrod?" Sarah asked.

For a moment I saw that old mischievous glint in her eye. The one that used to make her eyes sparkle all the time before she got sick.

"I could hardly believe it," I giggled. "It's hard to imagine old people young, you know it?"

Sarah paused, then whispered, "It's hard to imagine getting old. But I won't have to worry about that."

"Hey, kid," I broke in to lighten the moment, "take one day at a time."

"Yeah, right," she said, turning her face. A tear slid down her cheek.

Sometimes, no matter what kind of friends you are, there are some things best left alone. It wasn't one of those sobbing things. Sarah just needed to let a tear roll out for herself.

Enough of the sad stuff. I was about to cry myself. "Hey, Sarah, I gotta split."

"Call me later, will ya?" she asked.

"Sure," I grinned, giving her hand a squeeze.

As I was leaving I turned and said, "And tonight you better keep a watch on my house."

"No problem, my eye will be on the watch like the eye of the great pyramid." Sarah gave me a thumbs-up as I left.

It was kind of a running joke between us since she had the spyglass and watched all the houses around. Which was how she knew that the fourteen-year-old boy a couple of houses down lifted weights in his undies.

But I'll save that for another time. That was just girl talk and I was on my way home to monster-sit.

CHAPTER 14

Caller ID

By now Wily was worried sick. Poor Wily. He'd wanted to just be an anonymous prankster, hiding behind miles of phone lines. But it hadn't worked out that way.

My skunk brother was worried sick that the bikers at The Cave had his number. The only consolation was that they only had his phone number, not his address.

Like all sand-brained little kids, he figured he'd just answer all the calls that came into the house for the rest of his life. That way he'd be able to intercept the pool hall creeps and keep them from telling Mom and Dad about his bad phone habits.

My sister later told me how they took the phone number and found where we lived. They didn't have to call up and pretend to be delivering flowers, like the way they do it on *Matlock.* And they didn't have to pay someone off at the phone company to check our address like they do on the other detective shows.

No, it wasn't that these creeps were smart. When it came to brains, there wasn't more than one between them.

No, those pool hall dummies made wooden Indians look like Einsteins. But they did have enough smarts to call their boss. The bartender had called Mr. Seagel and told him that they had the kid's number. And you know what Seagel did? He didn't tell them to go research the area code. He didn't tell them to go house-to-house.

All he did was tell them to call the library. The *library* you say?

That's right. My sister says that crooks, cops, and collection agencies use the library all the time.

All they had to do was ask sweetly for someone to look in what's called the reverse directory. It's this book which lets you know who has what phone number.

It's really simple to use. And maybe in another book I'll tell you how I found where all the Orlando Magic players lived, just by writing down their phone numbers from a police security log book.

Yes, sir, that old reverse directory's pretty wild, but in the wrong hands, it's deadly. And the dirty, grimy hands of the creeps at The Cave were worse than deadly.

They were the real thing. Bone-crushing, face-stomping, back-breaking lunk-heads who ate kids like Wily for breakfast.

But I didn't know any of this. I was just heading home oblivious to it all, dreading the evening to come where I'd have to baby-sit for my brother.

It was at those times when I wished the moment my parents left, I'd turn into Dumbo and just sit on my brother all evening. Just sit, sit, sit, and squish, squish, squish. And if they found a flat-freckle monster cake on the floor when they got home, so be it.

But I wasn't Dumbo. I was just Patti "Pink" Pinkerton, all of about 90 pounds with blond, sometimes straight, sometimes styled hair, who likes to wear sunglasses.

I didn't know that goons knew our home phone number and address. Didn't know that they were planning on paying us a little visit so they could talk with the phone prankster.

But if I had, what could *I* have done? You got to take it as it comes. Any good detective knows that.

CHAPTER 15

Baby-sitting a Monst

"Are you sure you have to go out?" I asked my dad for the fifth time.

From the moment I'd gotten home it had been nonstop pestering. Usually, when you ask your parents the same thing over and over they give in. Not that you deserve what you want, but they just want to shut you up.

But my dad wasn't in a mood to give in. He wanted out of the house. I could tell the feeling that had come over him. Kids get hip to a parent's body language very quickly.

It was one of those days where he just wanted to be rid of the kids. Not that he didn't love us, because he did. But he just needed his own space.

"Patti, we're just going out to dinner," my dad said in exasperation.

"But what if something bad happens and..." I began, ready to pour out my usual doom and gloom list of things that could happen.

"Like what?" he sighed.

if Wily falls asleep
into his mouth and
he needs mouth-to-

his hand. "So give him

"W ach in his mouth?" I said with a look ense horror on my face.

"Just pull the cockroach out with your fingers, then give him mouth-to-mouth."

"But I hate cockroaches!"

"So use tweezers."

"But Dad, what if the cockroach has bitten into Wily's tonsils and won't let go?"

"No problem."

"No problem?" I asked in surprise.

My Dad grinned like the Cheshire cat. "Wily had his tonsils removed. Now you just relax, we won't be gone long."

He had me there. I forgot the kid had his tonsils pulled out. But my scenario wasn't strong enough to keep my parents home. I don't think a team of wild horses could have kept my father and mother from going out to eat.

It was with a sense of dread that I watched them get ready to leave.

My Dad was ready to go. "I called Domino's and ordered you one of those new big pizzas," he said proudly, like he was talking to the Teenage Mutant Ninja Turtles who would karate chop him if he hadn't ordered a big pizza.

"A Dominator?" my brother asked, which I guess was the name of their huge new pizza for pizza freaks.

"The biggest one they had," my dad grinned. "I left the money on the kitchen table." Then he looked at me. "Make sure you give the delivery boy a tip, okay."

"No problem."

"Don't stuff yourselves," my mom said. Just the thought of us eating too much made her nervous.

"We won't," I said, trying to put on a brave front. "You go out and enjoy yourselves."

They stepped out onto the porch. This was it, they were going to leave me with monster boy. "Have fun," I said.

"And call a cab if you need to," my brother said. My parents weren't drinkers, but my brother shouted it loud enough for the whole neighborhood to hear.

The two old ladies who Ramrod had chased were just shuffling by, moving their canes in unison. They tisk-tisked at my dad as if he drank too much.

I could see the look on my father's face, that I'll get you later, look. Why Wily always wanted to cause trouble, I'll never know. But I did know that monster boy was my responsibility for the next couple of hours.

Dad took his portable phone with him which was some peace of mind. It was my survival link in case Wily drove me nuts and off the deep end.

The moment they were out of sight, I heard a motorcycle engine crank up. It startled me but it made Wily fall to the ground like someone was shooting at him.

"What was that?" he gasped, looking around.

"Just a motorcycle," was all I said. Then I heard it again. It was coming from Ramrod's garage. In my mind I saw the old guy working on Gertie, tuning her engine and turning her on.

"Who is it?" Wily asked, looking like a scared rabbit.

"Mr. Carpenter has a Harley. I think he started it up."

Wily blew a long stream of air like he'd just survived a bungee jump. Something was out of whack but I couldn't figure out what.

Then he just blew me away. "I don't think I'm hungry," he said.

Now that might not seem unusual to *you*, but from Wily? That boy could eat the cardboard off the pizza box.

"You're not hungry?" I asked. "Are you sick?"

"Just not hungry," he said, and then he heard the phone ring and took off for it.

It was for me. "Patti, this is Sarah. Your parents just left, didn't they?"

"Yeah, left me with Wily Coyote," I groaned.

"Just checking," she whispered.

"Keep your eye on the 'hood," I said. Then she clicked off.

But just as I put the phone down, it rang again. "Pinkerton's," I said, like I was the butler or something.

"Is dis da Pinkerton's?" a gruff voice asked.

"Yeah, are you bringing the pizza now?" I asked, assuming it was Domino's. There was a pause on the line. "Hey," I said, not wanting to play phone games, "would you hurry up and bring the Dominator over."

Then I had a strange sensation. I could almost feel the voice grin on the line. "No problem. We'll be right over."

Little did I know that at the other end of the line were some of the thugs from The Cave. And the biggest one of the tattooed dumbos had a name on the back of his leather jacket written in blood-red letters:

DOMINATOR
DO OR DIE!

But oh no, my pea-brained brother didn't tell me his prank had backfired. He didn't tell me that the bullies down at The Cave knew our phone number, our names, and where we lived.

No, he had to cop out and tell me he wasn't hungry. The little creep just sat in the kitchen, acting scared.

"Are you sure you're not hungry?" I asked, trying to be the loving, caring sister I wasn't.

"Positive," he said.

Little did I know that the sound of Ramrod's cycle was being multiplied six times by the six leather-jacketed hoods walking out of The Cave.

Six guys who ate trash cans for dinner were on their way to our house. Six guys who would kidnap Santa and stuff him up a chimney. Six guys who would catch the Easter Bunny and eat him.

Yup, ol' Pink didn't know what was about to happen. I didn't know that they were coming over to see the punk who sent manure, flowers, and ambulances to their pool hall.

And I was baby-sitting the punk...a punk named Wily Pinkerton. My brother or maybe soon to be ex-brother.

CHAPTER 16

Dominator

The phone rang again but my brother grabbed it first. I was up in my attic domain, hacking away on my computer looking into files I wasn't supposed to.

"Who is this?" Wily asked loud enough for me to hear him from the kitchen.

Then I heard him confirm our pizza order which was kind of strange since I thought they'd just called. But this was *really* Domino's and not the bikers. So thinking back, I imagine my brother let out one long sigh of relief.

That was one phone call down and a million more to go for the rest of his life. I don't think it ever entered his head that he couldn't answer every call. But he was so desperate he would try anything to avoid telling Dad and Mom the truth about what he'd done.

Now we had the pizza guy and six bikers on their way over and my parents already gone to a fancy restaurant.

Then the phone rang again as I was coming down to the kitchen. Hacking into files was tiresome and made me hungry. The pizza would be arriving any moment and even though he said he wasn't hungry, I didn't want Wily to pull all the cheese off like he did the last time.

"We're all right, Mom," I heard Wily say.

My mom was already calling. While Wily was on the phone I heard the sound of more motorcycles. Wily hung up the phone and looked at me.

"Don't answer the door," he said.

"Why not? We've got a pizza coming."

"Just don't answer it. I'll throw the money out the window."

"You're acting stupid," I said.

Wily shook his head. "Never know when a mugger or thief might come to the door."

I walked away saying, "And you never know when your brother is going to be committed to the loony bin."

The sound of the cycles was getting closer. My brother broke out into a sweat.

"Is there something you're not telling me?" I asked. I was getting that creepy feeling that gives you goose bumps.

Then the sound of the cycles stopped. I figured that maybe Ramrod had called some old friends from a biker rest home and they had come to party.

I had to take the trash out so I went to the kitchen and picked up the bag while freckle-face stood there sweating. But as I closed the kitchen door behind me, I thought I heard it lock.

"Oh crud," I said, testing the handle.

It *was* locked. I was locked outside and Wily was going to be inside with the Dominator pizza. I pictured him dancing around the kitchen with all the cheese in his mouth, laughing at me.

The thought really burned me so I rushed to put the trash in the can. "I'll get in somehow," I muttered under my breath.

I knocked on the door and Wily popped his head up.

"Open the door. I'm locked out," I said, feeling stupid for having to state the obvious. "Open up."

"Knock knock," he said.

I looked at his face. I was so mad that his whole head seemed to be one big freckle waiting to be slapped.

"*I'm* supposed to say knock, knock. I'm locked out."

"Knock, knock." he insisted.

"Who's there?" I asked disgustedly.

"Password."

I saw the look in his eye and knew what he was getting to. "Password who?"

"Tell me the password to your room and I'll let you in."

I started to tell him just to get him to open the door, but the doorbell rang. "I'll go around the front and get the pizza," I said.

"No! I've got the money," Wily said. He was all nervous again.

The doorbell rang once again and my brother was shaking in his shorts. "Don't answer it. We don't need to eat. Pizza is fattening anyway."

I looked at him. His legs were crossed, his arms were crossed and his eyes were crossed. He had lost his marbles.

"Let me in. I'm hungry," I said, rattling the door back and forth.

But Wily was determined to hold off fate. He ran to the front door and stood in front of it like he was trying to hold back the tide.

He ran back and whispered, "It might be a mugger." The doorbell rang out again.

"And it might be the man with our Dominator," I said. "I'll go around front and get it."

Wily's face went white. "Let me answer it, okay?" he said, looking at me with wide eyes.

"Why?" I asked, tired of his game. All I wanted was to get back inside.

"Because you're a girl and I want to protect you."

"Poof." I dismissed him.

"Please," he whispered, like it was the most important thing in his life.

"Okay," I said disgustedly. "But let me in and bring the pizza to the kitchen."

"I'll be right back," he nodded, like a zombie.

Little did I know who was waiting out front.

This is what happened as best I can figure.

Wily must have felt like Little Red Riding Hood. There was someone at the door and he was worried that it was someone from the you-know-where. "Who's there?" he whispered through the door.

"Dominator," said a gruff voice.

Wily, thinking it was the pizza man, opened the door. "Here's the money," he started to say, then stopped.

It wasn't the pizza man standing there. It wasn't even the pizza boy standing there.

No, standing in front of Wily was somebody bigger than Hulk Hogan, meaner than Jason and badder than Freddy.

"Wh-who are you?" Wily shook.

"I'm Dominator. We come to have a little talk with you."

Wily did what any red-blooded American Clint Eastwood fan would do. He slammed the door.

"Open up, punk!" Dominator shouted.

"Go away," Wily screamed.

The Dominator kicked at the door. "Open it up or I'll knock it down!"

I guess the closed door was like talking on the phone, because my brother went nuts. "You can huff and puff all you want but you ain't gettin' in." Wily was on a roll. "You're lower than alligator slime you bunch of losers."

"Did you hear what he said?" one of the biker bums asked Dominator.

"Yeah, I heard," the big dummy said, making a fist. The Dominator had to act or be laughed at. "Let's do it," he growled, lifting back his foot to kick in the door.

"My sister's a cop!" Wily shouted.

"Then bring your sister out here!" the Dominator shouted back. From the look on his face you could tell he wanted to chew on some concrete to calm down.

Now I didn't know what the heck was going on. All I knew was that I was still locked out, Wily was inside and the pizza was outside. I didn't want Wily to pull off all the cheese, so I had to do something.

Seeing Wily standing inside the house talking through the closed door led my detective brain to deduce that the pizza was still on the front porch. So I went around to the front of the house to try and get the Dominator before Wily got it.

CHAPTER 17

Worst Nightmare

I heard the phone ring as I walked past the kitchen window on the side of the house. Wily was inside and answered it.

Though I couldn't hear what he was saying, I could tell by the way he rolled his eyes that it was Mom calling. It was something Wily always did behind her back when she was worrying unnecessarily again.

But this is how Wily said the call went down.

"Pinkertons."

"Wily, this is your mom. Is everything okay?"

In the background, the Dominator was kicking at the door. Evidently my Mom could hear it over the phone.

"Yeah, Mom, everything's fine."

"What's that noise?"

"It's someone at the door."

"Has the Dominator arrived?" my dad said loud enough for Wily to hear.

Wily looked towards the door which was being pounded on. "Oh yeah, the Dominator has arrived," he said, which was the understatement of the year.

"Okay, well I was just checking," my mom said.

Wily hung up and began to cry. What was he to do? He had a group of blood-crazed bikers trying to knock down the door because of the illegal prank calls he made and if he told Dad, he'd get punished. It was a no-win situation of the worst kind.

But I didn't know any of this. I was just the sweet, innocent, thirteen-year-old girl who was about to run headlong into a bunch of bikers who had more than "momma" tattooed on their arms.

As I came around to the front door I stopped. There were big motorcycles parked in front of our house. Six of them.

They weren't parked down at Ramrod's. They were parked in front of *our* house. I could hear the sound of neighbors bolting their front doors up and down the neighborhood. Oh, oh.

The bikers saw *me* before I saw *them.*

"Are you the sister?" someone asked with a

slight whistle. I looked up and saw a stubble-faced clod with a broken nose, grinning with his tongue sticking out through his missing front teeth. How he could eat anything tougher than baby food was beyond me.

"Sister of who?" I asked. It didn't take this detective long to figure out that these guys weren't bringing pizza.

"Sister of the punk inside the house," another biker said.

I love George Washington and believe in telling the truth, but not this time. "I live over there," I said, pointing to Sarah's house.

"Kick the door down," biker number three said.

Then I focused on the biggest one. The one who had arms the size of butcher shop slabs of beef. Hands the size of hams. Legs the size of telephone poles.

On the back of his jacket was written, Dominator. I know my Domino's pizza. And this was no Dominator.

But they weren't going to bother me. They wanted Wily and I wanted out of there. So I started to go across the street to Sarah's. I would have made it, too, if Wily hadn't opened the window.

"Patti, call the cops! Help!"

I looked back. Wily's eyes were bulging out.

"Who's that?" Dominator asked Wily.

"That's my sister," Wily screamed. He picked the worst moment to suddenly start telling the truth.

"Smallest cop I've ever seen," Dominator said, scratching his head.

"Cop's a cop," biker number four growled.

"Who are you guys?" I asked. "It's a little early for Halloween," I said, trying to test their sense of humor.

But when these guys were born they didn't get any funny bones.

"It ain't Halloween," the biker missing teeth said.

"Get 'em, Patti!" my unhelpful brother screamed as he slammed the window closed.

They started off the porch toward me but I was saved by the bell. Well, not exactly the bell, but close enough. A pizza truck actually.

The Domino's pizza truck pulled up, catching the bikers off guard. I went into action as Patti "Pink" Pinkerton, thirteen-year-old would-be detective. I rolled into the bushes.

I don't think Jessica on *Murder She Wrote* did it this way, but I wasn't too proud to crawl through the bushes to escape.

But the poor pizza guy, he was probably used to delivering to all kinds of creeps and weirdos. He just adjusted his pizza hat and got out of the truck carrying our Dominator pizza. And he was heading straight for the Dominator himself.

CHAPTER 18

Call the Cops

Luckily, Sarah was watching from across the street and she called my house. Unluckily, freckle-head answered.

"Wily, this is Sarah. What's going on over there?" she asked. She'd seen the bikers on the porch and me crawling away and knew that this wasn't a surprise slumber party.

"Call the cops!" Wily screamed and slammed the phone down. One of the bikers was now trying to open the front porch window. Wily hid in the closet. I crept in through the basement.

I looked around for a weapon and then saw the cat box in the corner. I picked it up and ran over to the window.

"Here, kitty, kitty," I called out. The biker looked up and I dumped the cat box down on his face.

"I'll get you, sister!" the biker shouted.

Sarah told me later that she sat there trying to figure out what to do. So she did the obvious and called the police. My sister, to be exact.

"Carol Pinkerton please," she said, calling the number I'd given her in case there was ever an emergency.

When my sister came on, Sarah got right to the point and told her what was up. That I was baby-sitting monster-boy and a group of bikers were assaulting the house like it was the Alamo. Sarah kept her spyglass trained on my front yard as she talked.

"Where are they now?" Carol asked.

Sarah moved her spyglass around. "Bad guys in the front yard, good guys inside."

"Hmm," my sister said, very profoundly. Then she heard Sarah gasp and asked, "Where are they now?"

"They're in the backyard and the front."

"Keep watching," my sister said. "We're on our way."

"Hurry," Sarah said, moving her spyglass back and forth to keep up with all the action.

"And, Sarah, call my dad's portable phone," my sister said, hanging up. Carol knew that Sarah always had that number in case she needed help.

Sarah sat there trying to figure out what to do. The police were on their way, so everything was going to be all right. But she didn't want to call my parents. She knew that they'd come unglued.

Meanwhile, the bikers were assaulting the house.

The pizza man kept asking for his money. "The guy inside has it," the bikers said, pointing to Wily whose face was scrunched against the window glass.

Wily opened the window and threw the money out.

"What about a tip?"

"Tip?" Wily asked, wondering how the guy had the nerve to ask with all that going on.

"Yeah, you know, for delivering this pizza," he said, holding up the box.

"My tip to you," Wily shouted, "is to take the money and run."

But the pizza man was stubborn. "Everyone always gives me a tip."

But he said this just as Dominator was coming around the corner. "You want a tip?" the big lunk-head asked.

"Yeah," the stubborn pizza guy said.

"Well, tip over," Dominator said, shoving the guy over like a domino.

Dominator grabbed the pizza box before it hit the ground and began stuffing the pizza into his mouth. Then he stared back at us with runny cheese and tomato sauce dripping down his chest. It looked straight out of a slasher movie.

I heard the phone ring. Wily answered it and held it up. "It's for you. It's Sarah."

"Tell her I'm busy."

One of the bikers took off his belt. "Tell her she's tied up right now."

"Or about to be," grunted another one.

I opened the window above the sink and stuck Wily's boom box on the ledge. I pressed "play" and strange sounds started blaring out.

It was like Def Leppard, Beethoven, Mr. Rogers and Mr. Ed had all gotten together and recorded a song. Wily couldn't figure it out.

Then it dawned on him. It was the gator mating call tape that my sister had brought over.

"What kind of music is that?" Dominator asked.

"Don't sound like rap music to me," the toothless wonder grunted, trying to move to the gator grunts.

Then I heard the sounds of the troops arriving. Not the police. Not the neighbors. No. The grunting sounds I heard coming from the backyard were a dozen gators, led by old Randy himself.

I guess the bikers looked like leather gators.

"Good luck, gator bait!" Wily screamed to the bikers. "Hope you know how to do the crocodile rock!"

Then we heard a loud commotion in the backyard. The gators and bikers were about to slam dance.

CHAPTER 19

Battle Gear

Dominator was moving around between the gators like he had ants in his pants. "Down boy," he shouted, as each one of the green monsters took a nip at him.

The toothless biker climbed up the tetherball pole and clung on for dear life. Below him sat another gator, looking up with adoring eyes.

"Think we should turn the tape off?" my brother asked.

"No," I said. "Let's turn it louder."

As my fingers turned up the volume, I wondered if I'd ever feel safe in the house after dark again.

I went about the kitchen like I was one of the Fantastic Four getting ready for battle. I started water boiling and told monster boy to take out a dozen eggs from the refrigerator, and get out tomatoes, potatoes, and anything else that would fit into the palm of his hand.

Then I turned and whispered, "Let's get our battle gear on."

While the house was under siege, my parents were at a restaurant, trying to relax. But my mother had mother's intuition and wanted my father to call home once again. This is how my father later said the conversation went.

My mother looked at her watch. "You better call home and see how the kids are doing."

"But I've already called them two times. They're fine."

Mother took a deep breath. "I just feel that something's wrong."

"How about a glass of wine to calm you down?" my father asked.

But my mother shook her head. She didn't drink and didn't want to start now. "Just call once more and I'll be satisfied."

So my father called and that's when Wily picked up the phone. Actually, Wily picked up the phone just as one of the bikers tried to climb through the kitchen window and I slammed it down on his fingers.

There was a loud scream in the background as Wily said, "Hello."

"Wily? What was that noise?" my father asked. "Where's your sister?"

"Right here," he said handing me the phone as I carried in a bag of stuff and two GI Joe commando battle belts.

"Is everything all right?" my father asked.

"Patti, I asked if anything was wrong?" my father asked again.

I thought. Gee Dad, there's six bikers who want to kill us out in the backyard with a pack of starving gators behind them, but other than that, there's nothing wrong.

So I did what I thought best and continued fibbing. I played with the truth. "Everything's fine."

"Why are you playing the music so loud? Is anyone else there?"

"No one else is in the house," I said, which was the truth. Sure, there were bikers *outside*, but just Wily and I were *in* the house.

But not for long. I looked up and saw Dominator looking through the door. His clothes were in tatters and he was dragging an alligator behind him.

"Gotta run, Dad, the Dominator is here," I said, not thinking about what I was saying.

"Oh good," my father said. "Now go eat your pizza. We'll be home soon."

I hung up the phone and Wily tapped me on the shoulder. "Let's go," I said.

I turned and said, "Here's your chance to be a real GI Joe."

"No—it's time to surrender."

"No way," I said, handing him a battle gear belt.

"I took these from your room. These bags are filled with your itching powder, these are the smoke bombs, here are cherry bombs and the glass vials are the stink bombs."

"Stink bombs?" he asked, taking one out of the bullet holder.

The Dominator was impatient. "Open the door!" he commanded. Behind him stood the five bikers. All their clothes were ripped.

"I think they're looking for Macaulay Culkin, not us," Wily said. He was in an obvious state of denial.

Then I heard a scraping sound and looked towards the open kitchen window. Fingers were on the windowsill, trying to climb up.

"To the ramparts!" I screamed as if I was back in King Arthur's castle.

I took the boiling pot of water off the stove and poured it down onto the guy at the window. Ouch! The other bikers ran over to help their parboiled friend, who was now being pursued by a gator.

We started tossing the eggs, tomatoes and potatoes down on them. While this was going on, the Dominator just stood at the door and stared in at us through the glass top-half. His face was growing madder and madder by the second.

Then the phone rang again. It was my sister calling on her portable phone. "What the heck's going on over there?" she asked.

"Six bikers are trying to break into the house."

"Just stay inside. We'll be right there," she said, hanging up.

Oh what a bogus baby-sitting job this was turning out to be! Here I was supposed to have a quiet evening with Wily while we ate our Dominator pizza. Now the Dominator ate our pizza and wanted to eat us!

I looked out the window and saw that the bikers had regrouped and were preparing to ram the door. All I needed were my parents to come home and find the house trashed.

"We got to get outta here," Wily said.

"We're safer in here," I said, dropping an iron skillet out the window on one of the biker's heads. The clunking sound was so loud that I hoped Mom's skillet wasn't dented.

"But they'll trash the house!"

"Well?" I shrugged. "That's what insurance is for."

"If they wreck the house we'll never get allowance for the rest of our lives." he said.

I thought about that for a nanosecond, then nodded. "Let's go," I said.

We both turned and looked at the Dominator's face pressed against the glass.

"Front door!" we both shouted and hightailed it down the hall.

We were surrounded by bikers!

I ran to the stereo, switched it on, and pulled a small microphone from its back and shouted into it, "This is the cops. We've got the place surrounded. You creeps have had it."

It was connected to a speaker hooked up in the garage.

"That should drive them from the backyard," he nodded. We saw three of them run alongside the house.

"Side door," Wily whispered, and took off towards the sun room off the living room.

No one was there, so we opened the door and looked around. "The coast is clear," I whispered.

We started toward the front of the house to see if they'd left, but Toothless stepped out. "Come to poppa," he smiled.

"Moonwalk retreat," my brother said, and backpeddled like Michael Jackson toward the garage.

But when we got there we ran head-on into two other bikers. If they hadn't been so mauled from the gators they would have caught us, but we were faster.

Between running from the bikers and dodging gators, we barely made it to the garage, where we found ourselves trapped. Trapped like rats in a trap. Like roaches in a Roach Motel.

"What are we going to do?" Wily asked.

"Prepare arms," I whispered, pulling out a smoke bomb. He lit the thing and I tossed it toward the bikers, but the wind blew the smoke back at us.

"Now what?" he asked as we coughed.

"Operation FOJ."

"FOJ?"

"Yeah, Fourth Of July," I grinned, taking out a cherry bomb.

Now I knew that cherry bombs were illegal, but at that exact moment, I didn't care if it was a federal crime. I watched as Wily lit the fuse and I tossed it.

The noise was loud enough to be heard coast-to-coast but it knocked the bikers back. Which brought the gators back after them.

"Let's go," I said, pulling Wily toward my dad's golf cart.

Now, I don't know about you, but I'd never heard of anyone escaping from a bunch of angry bikers in a golf cart, but it wasn't the time to be choosy and I had to improvise.

"You got the key?" Wily asked.

"I'll just hotwire it," I said, reaching down and twisting a few wires.

I grabbed a bag of nails from Dad's workbench and stood alongside the less-than-fast golf cart. "Open the garage door," I said.

We lurched out of the garage. It was like something right out of the movies. I maneuvered the cart through the bikers, over two gators and then laid golf cart rubber around the side of the house and jumped the curb in the front.

"Where'd you learn to drive like that?" he asked, holding on.

"Nintendo," I replied.

"Right," he grinned.

I looked back and saw Dominator coming. The alligators were still chasing him.

"Dominator's coming! Hit the gas!" Wily shouted.

"This thing's electric," I said.

"Then turn on the juice and move it." Dominator was heading toward his motorcycle.

"Where should we go?" I asked.

"I don't want to play nine holes," he said. Now the other bikers were getting on their Harleys.

We heard the sound of motorcycles starting. "Let's head for downtown Winter Park," I said, like that was entering a United Nations peacekeeping zone or someplace where we'd be safe.

Wily saw the bikers coming toward us. "We're dead." That's all he said. *We're dead.* "Faster!" he screamed.

"Say your prayers," I said. "Dad's golf cart only goes five miles an hour. I estimate that those Harleys can do about 200 so they'll catch up to us in about twenty feet."

Then we heard the police sirens in the distance. "Here comes the cavalry!"

"And here comes the enemy," Wily said. I could see the expression on Dominator's face. He was not a happy camper.

"They're coming fast," Wily said. "We're dead, we are. We're dead, dead, *dead*."

I looked back and saw the The Cave goons just a half block away.

"They look like they've got an attitude about all this," I sighed.

"A bad attitude," Wily said. "We need a miracle quick or they're gonna nail us."

"That's it!" I shouted. I opened the bag of nails and poured them onto the street behind us.

But the police cars came careening out from a side street and followed right behind us...right over the nails. As their tires blew out I whispered, "We're in trouble now."

"Big trouble," Wily agreed. "Like death penalty trouble I think," he whispered.

"Oh, oh," Wily said, nodding with his head.

Dominator was wise to my trick. He maneuvered around the nails by riding up the sidewalk.

We managed to elude the bikers by going up driveways and across front lawns until we got to the golf course. I headed straight toward the fifth green, which would take us into the business district where we would lose the lunatic bikers for sure.

What a horrible night this had turned out to be so far. I was supposed to be home baby-sitting and here I was trying to escape blood-thirsty bikers in Dad's golf cart. The nails I'd dropped had flattened the police tires and we'd left a bunch of crazy gators doing the crocodile rock in our backyard.

I tried to block out the image of Wily and me spending the rest of our lives in the same prison cell. That would not be Patti's excellent adventure by any stretch of the imagination.

CHAPTER 20

Street Fight

Back on my street, my sister and the other police checked out the house. "No one's here," the lieutenant said to my sister.

"I knew that was them," she sighed. Carol had seen the golf cart going down the street. "That had to be my sister driving."

"How old is she?"

"You don't want to know," she sighed. *They'll never outrun those bikers*, she thought to herself.

"What the heck is that grunting noise?" the Lieutenant asked, scratching his head.

"Beats me," Carol said, then stopped. "The tape," she mumbled.

"Hey, back here!" a policeman screamed. They'd found the gators. It was all they could do to drive them from the backyard.

Meanwhile, Wily and I were cruising down the middle of Park Avenue in downtown Winter Park, trying to escape. "Think we lost 'em?" Wily asked.

"I hope so."

Then we saw Dominator coming at us from the opposite direction!

"Wily, I'm going to stop here!" I said. I brought the golf cart to a halt. "I'm getting out. Take over."

"Where're you going?" he asked.

"Throw one of your smoke bombs, then head back and get Ramrod."

"Who?" Wily asked.

"Mr. Carpenter. Tell him that the bikers are after us and we need his help."

"You sure?"

"Positive," I said.

I needed to lead the bikers away from Dad's golf cart and Wily, who I was supposed to be baby-sitting. Wily ignited a smoke bomb and tossed it in the street. The smoke was so thick that I could hardly see my brother.

"Now go," I said.

"Good luck," Wily said, driving the wrong way down a one way street. At this point, we'd broken so many laws that another moving violation wouldn't matter much.

I used the cover of the smoke bomb to lose myself in the crowd of Park Avenue shoppers.

Dominator must have been wise to my trick, because first I saw his parked bike and then saw him coming toward me through the crowd. He stood head and shoulders above the rest. Like a professional basketball player at a daycare center.

The other bikers were covering the side streets so I had no choice but to keep going. I went through a department store, a sushi restaurant and an ice cream shop. But the Dominator kept coming.

Then I heard the train coming. It was my only hope! I dashed between the cars on Park Avenue and headed across the park with Dominator in close pursuit. He was carrying his Harley! Like it was made out of papier-mâché!

The southbound train pulled into the station for its two-minute Winter Park stop. "All aboard," the conductor shouted.

You needed a ticket to get on the train, and I didn't have one. But I did have a *need* to get on that train, so I did what great-great-grandpa Pinkerton would have done. I snuck on!

I saw a woman get off the train and buy a paper from the newsbox, then climb back on. I followed right on her heels.

"You got a ticket?" the conductor asked.

"My mother's got it," I said, smiling as sweetly as I could.

The engineer blasted the whistle. It was time to move on. The conductor shook his head. "Next time, bring your ticket with you if you get off."

"I will, sir," I said sweetly, climbing on the train. I took a seat by the window which was a mistake. When I looked outside, Dominator was looking in at me.

He was scrunching his face on the glass again which must have been something he liked to do. But it sure left the window yucky.

I looked out and the other five bikers pulled up. Dominator pointed behind the train and they took off. Then I heard the police sirens as the train began moving.

The train jolted forward as the conductor climbed back on. Dominator lifted his Harley onto the train then pulled himself up.

"Your ticket, please," the conductor said, not wanting to offend the meanest looking man he'd ever seen.

Dominator held out his fist. The conductor looked at it, thought about how his jaw would feel against the fist, then shrugged and moved on.

My goose was cooked! The Dominator was on the train with me! I had no choice. I moved toward the back of the train.

I looked out as we passed through Winter Park. Little did I know that the bikers had managed to mount their tires on the track by letting a little air out and were following right behind! And behind them were the police who had driven onto the rails.

It was all right out of a movie except I didn't have the buttered popcorn!

"Next stop, downtown Orlando," the conductor shouted.

I did my best to keep ahead of the biker beast, but the Dominator kept on coming like he was the battery bunny. Every train car he walked through went dead quiet. Of course

I'd shut up too if I saw a guy the size of Hulk Hogan pushing a Harley down the aisle.

There was only so far I could go and finally I reached the last car. I went out onto the platform and looked back. Coming down the tracks were the five bikers and behind them, two police cars.

Then I felt hands of steel grab my left arm. The Dominator had me.

I bent my head back and looked up, and up and up until I saw his face. This thirteen-year-old would-be detective needed an idea fast.

We were going through downtown Orlando and it was the last stop before Tampa. So I said, "Hi, Mr. Dominator," while reaching up with my left hand to pull the emergency-stop cord.

The train came to a screeching stop so fast that Dominator fell down and the bikers behind us crashed into the rear of the train. Then the police cars following behind them crashed and well...it was some mess.

But what did I care? I vaulted over the rail and ran for my life toward the bright lights of Orlando.

CHAPTER 21

Church Street Showdown

Ramrod looked at my brother. "Do you have a license to drive that thing?"

Wily shrugged. "It's my dad's golf cart."

"That ain't what I asked."

Wily started to be flippant, then stopped. This wasn't old Mr. Carpenter, the crazy neighbor he was talking to. No, this was *Ramrod.*

"No, I don't," Wily admitted.

"I thought so," Ramrod said, pushing his Harley out of the garage.

Wily couldn't believe it was the same man. It was an amazing transformation. Like Clark Kent to Superman. Ramrod was decked out in black leather pants, white T-shirt, his hair (or what was left of it) slicked back and something was rolled up in his sleeve.

"Are those cigarettes?" Wily asked, pointing to the lump in the sleeve.

"Nah," Ramrod said, "I gave up smoking twenty years ago. But it looks better this way so I rolled up a small box of M&Ms to look tough."

Wily couldn't help but grin. "You better hurry," he said.

"Where were they headed?"

"Last I saw her, she was heading toward the train," Wily said.

Ramrod put on his black leather jacket, zipped up the four zippers, buttoned the twenty buttons, then put on his shades and his helmet.

"But it's dark already, Mr. Carpenter."

"Name's *Ramrod*, boy."

"But it's nighttime, Ramrod."

"I'll be all right," Ramrod said. He cranked up Gertie and she roared to life.

"Where are you going?" Wily asked.

"To The Cave. That's where this whole thing will end."

"But that's a biker bar," Wily exclaimed.

"And I'm an old biker," Ramrod nodded. "See you later, alligator," he said, peeling down the driveway.

"I hope Pink's alright," Wily whispered, watching him zoom away.

Little did he know that at that exact moment I was running for my life through Orlando's downtown tourist spot called Church Street Station. Luckily there were hundreds of people on the street or Dominator would have nabbed me for sure.

But I was quick as a bunny and kept one step ahead by sneaking under tables and hiding behind waiters.

When I got to the disco, things really got out of hand. Well, to be more exact, there were a lot of groping hands. "Hey, babe, you want to dance?" a dork asked me.

Then, from out of nowhere, the Dominator stepped out. "She saved the last dance for me," he said, showing me his teeth or what was left of them.

"Dance with this," I said, taking out a stinkbomb and throwing it at his feet.

Chaos erupted! Everyone began running around holding their noses. "What's that smell?" a dozen people screamed.

"Him!" I shouted, pointing to Dominator.

I guess he was embarrassed because he spun around looking ill at ease. I used the opportunity to run to the taxi stand and flag a cab. The only problem was that there was another passenger already inside.

"I've got another fare already," the cab driver said.

"Where you going?" the man in the back asked.

"To Winter Park," I said.

The passenger tapped the cab driver. "You can drop me off along the way." He turned to me. "Get in, I'll cover your fare."

What a deal! I got in and closed the door. He was a nice-looking older man, about Ramrod's age. "Thank you very much."

"You're welcome, young lady. Glad to help."

At the next corner we passed by the five bikers who were still looking for me. They looked all busted up but I wasn't sure if that was from dancing with the gators or crashing off the train tracks. As we turned to make the light, Dominator ran out and stuck his face against the window, but the cab was gone before he could do anything.

I sat back and let out a deep sigh of relief. A dozen police cars whizzed past. I was saved.

"Where are you going?" I asked the man.

"To The Cave," the man said. "My name's Jack Seagel. What's yours?"

I closed my eyes. I was riding in a cab with Ramrod's old biker friend. The one who owned The Cave. The one my sister wanted to arrest.

My detective skills amazed even me! I hadn't even been on the case for a day and already I had captured the biggy...well almost.

CHAPTER 22

Collision Course

This is what I pieced together after it all happened. When Wily got home, he did more work around the house than he'd done in his whole life. He cleaned off the windows and swept the stairs. He hosed off the yard.

He didn't do this because he was a good boy. No, Wily Pinkerton worked fast and furious because he wanted to hide all the evidence. He didn't want Mom or Dad to know that anything had happened at the house.

Then the phone rang. Wily debated whether to answer it or not. *What if it's those guys and they're holding Patti hostage?* he wondered.

He should have rushed to the phone to see if I was all right, but he didn't. Wily just kicked his shoes against the kitchen table, trying to decide if he should answer it or not.

"What I don't know won't hurt me," he decided.

But it wasn't the bikers on the phone, it was Sarah. She was calling to warn Wily that our parents were driving down the street.

Sarah knew that I wasn't home yet. She'd seen both of us leave in the golf cart but only Wily return. So she did what any good, self-respecting friend would do and tried to cover for me.

I'd given her my father's portable phone number in case of emergencies, so Sarah dialed it. "Mr. Pinkerton? This is Sarah. Would you go to the drugstore up the street and pick up my medicine?"

My dad took the bait and turned around in the driveway and went back toward the drugstore. Sarah called Wily again and this time he answered but didn't say anything.

"Wily, I know you're there. This is Sarah. Talk to me!"

"What do you want?" Wily whispered.

"Did you see your parents just drive up?"

"Yeah," Wily said quietly, "and then they drove away which will give me more time to clean the place up."

"Where's Pink?"

"She's on a train heading toward Tampa."

"To Tampa!" Sarah exclaimed.

"That's where I last saw her. Gotta go, bye," Wily said, and hung up. It dawned on him that I was probably gone for good and that he'd inherit my attic room. Nice brother, eh?

I'll turn it into my TV room, a place where me and the guys can hang out. Then he frowned. *'Course I'll have to paint it another color. I hate pink.*

So while Wily was mapping out everything he wanted to do in the attic now that he figured I was gone, Dominator and the five bikers were busy trying to flag down cars. They wanted to get back to The Cave fast, but all their motorcycles had been wrecked when the train stopped.

Hidden in an alley was my sister, Officer Carol Pinkerton who hoped they would lead her to me. Her plan was to follow them in the squad car, even though it didn't go very fast with a bent frame.

Dominator just hoped he'd be the first to wring my neck. He had jumped off the train to chase me and had left his Harley on the train. Now he was a bikeless biker looking for a lift.

The bikers flagged down a truck. Dominator climbed up on the truck step. "Take us to The Cave," he growled.

"I'm goin' right by there," the truck driver said.

"I'll sit next to you," Dominator said, opening the door. He turned to the other bikers. "Climb up on the back, boys."

The driver waited until the other bikers were on, then drove slowly away.

Carol followed behind them in her banged up squad car that looked like it had been tossed by a tornado. She had to follow three blocks behind because her engine sounded like a garbage disposer with rocks in it. How she was going to explain the damage to her captain was not something she wanted to think about.

My whole world was on a collision course. The owner of The Cave and I were heading to the club. Ramrod was heading to the club. Dominator and the five bikers were heading to the club. And following behind them was my policewoman sister.

A good detective assembles the facts, clues and suspects, but you got to admit, I was out-doing myself bringing them all together at one time!

CHAPTER 23

Ramrod to the Rescue

"Okay, kiddo," Jack Seagel said to me as he got out of the cab at The Cave, "you're on your own."

He tipped the driver a twenty dollar bill. "You make sure she gets home safe and sound, you hear me?" The cab driver nodded.

"Thanks, Mr. Seagel," I smiled. He winked and walked off toward the club. It was hard to be mad at a guy who had just paid your cab fare.

Then I smelled something and crinkled my nose. The cab driver shook his head. "I hate driving behind diesel exhaust."

A truck had pulled up beside us. It was generating enormous plumes of thick black smoke.

"Roll your window up," the cabbie said. "That truck stinks."

"Okay," I said. I hadn't figured out my plan for solving the case but I knew it would come to me.

I tried to roll the window up but it didn't seem to go anywhere. Then I saw the hand holding the window down. Not just any hand, but a hand that Bigfoot would be proud to call his own.

"Get outta the cab," said a familiar deep voice. It was Dominator, and he wasn't looking to share a cab ride.

I heard a cycle pull in on the other side of the truck and just figured it was another biker. Little did I know it was Ramrod.

The old biker got off his Harley and walked slowly toward the front door. The bouncer looked him up and down. "What you want, Pops?"

"Is Jack Seagel here?"

"Who's askin'?" the bouncer said. He was so big, fat, and hairy that he could have been Santa's evil twin.

But Ramrod wasn't in the mood to be messed with. "Tell him Ramrod's here."

"Ramrod?" the bouncer questioned, as if the name were supposed to mean something but it didn't.

"Yeah, I own half this joint so you better move it."

While this was going on, my sister cruised slowly into the parking lot. If her engine hadn't sounded like a lawn mower running over rocks, she might have snuck in unnoticed. But not this time.

"It's the cops!" the toothless biker exclaimed.

Dominator yanked at the cab's door and pulled it off. "Get out," he ordered.

The cabbie looked at the door in Dominator's hands. "Yeah, *please*, get out," he said to me.

Carol saw me and jumped out of her squad car. "Back off!" she shouted at Dominator.

I took the opportunity to slide out the other door. "Get her!" Dominator screamed. The five bikers started after me.

"Stop or I'll shoot!" Carol screamed and the bikers froze in place. It was an adult version of Red Light-Green Light with me as the booby prize.

The driver pulled his truck forward to unload. I watched him go about his business like it was no big deal that a cop and six bikers were about to get into it.

Then I saw Ramrod standing at the door of the club, arguing with the man who paid my cab fare. Ramrod was holding up a piece of paper. My detective's sixth sense told me it had to be the IOU.

"You never paid me back," Ramrod said.

Jack Seagel looked at the note and then at Ramrod. "I thought you'd disappeared."

"Nope. Just changed my life and went straight. Like you should," Ramrod nodded.

"Run, Patti!" my sister cried out.

I turned to see Dominator bearing down on me. My feet went into overdrive and I headed toward the side of the building.

About twenty bikers came out from the side door. "Get her!" Dominator shouted, and they all came after me.

All I could do was run. I didn't have a plan, I didn't have a clue and I was scared silly. How would you feel if twenty mean thugs were after you?

I reached into my GI Joe commando belt and began tossing stink bombs behind me. The stink managed to slow down all the bikers except for Dominator, who kept coming forward.

I saw a trash dumpster and came up with a quick plan. I climbed up on the dumpster, opened up all the packets of itching powder and waited until the Dominator came around the corner.

Then with precision accuracy befitting a Top Gun, I dropped the itching powder on Dominator's head. In a blink he was rolling around on the ground like a dog with an itch.

Luck wasn't on my side. I ran back to where my sister was and collided with the pack of bikers. They'd recovered from my stink-bomb attack.

"There she is!" the big, ugly one shouted.

I ran toward where the trucker was busy unloading his cargo. I was able to slip around him but the herd of bikers came barreling around the corner and knocked him over spilling his cargo: 500 gallons of dark, gooey, sticky cola syrup.

Ramrod called to Carol and me. He wanted me to come meet the new owner of The Cave. Himself!

"Jack may be a crook, but he's paid his debt to me in full."

"What?" we both said.

"He's ripped up the IOU. I own the place. He said, 'It's not worth the trouble'."

My sister was smiling. "Is that okay with you, Sis?" I asked.

"It's not up to me," she said, then turned to Ramrod. "You shouldn't have a problem getting a license in your name for this place. But you ought to change its name...and the clientele."

Ramrod grinned. "I was thinking about Patti's Place."

"You can't call a pool hall Patti's Place," Mr. Seagel exclaimed.

"Why not?" Ramrod shrugged. "It's my place, ain't it."

I smiled at Ramrod. "I think you should call it Ramrod's Place."

Carol looked at her watch and whistled. "You better get home. Dad will flip out if he finds you gone."

"How am I gonna get there?" I asked.

Ramrod stepped forward. "Get on Gertie."

"She doesn't have a helmet," Carol warned.

Mr. Seagel smiled. "Take one of theirs," he said, handing me one from a parked bike.

"What about them?" I asked, pointing to the bikers who were lying in the sticky pool of syrup.

"I need to hose them off before I can arrest them," she grinned.

I climbed on the back of the big Harley and rode home with Ramrod. So far this had been a great first day on the job!

CHAPTER 24

Home Again

Back on the home front, Sarah was keeping watch. When she saw my parents coming down the street, she dialed Dad on the portable phone.

"Mr. Pinkerton, this is Sarah and..."

My father was grumpy. "Sarah, we got your medicine and..."

"And I was just wondering if you'd do me a favor and get some fresh orange juice from the grocery store for me. I need it to take my medicine with it."

"All right," my father said, turning the car around.

Sarah saved the day because Ramrod and I passed them as they drove down the street. I started to wave but Ramrod stopped me.

"They'll never recognize you," he said, gunning the engine.

Ramrod drove his Harley up to the front door and let me off. "What they don't know won't hurt 'em," he winked, then gunned the engine and drove off doing a wheelie.

I ran up the porch stairs and banged on the door. "Wily, Wily, let me in!"

Wily popped his head up behind the glass. "Not by the hair on my chinny-chin-chin."

I was in no mood for games. "Open the door, Wily. Mom and Dad will be here in a second."

"What's the password?" he asked.

"I won't tell you," I said, disgustedly.

"No, what's *my* password," he grinned. "See if you like how it feels."

I looked at him long and hard then whispered in an icy, ominous tone, "Wily Pinkerton, if you don't open the door now I'm going to smash all your video games."

"You wouldn't," he whispered, eyes wide.

"Try me," I said.

That got him. He opened the door and I stepped inside. But before I could even turn around I heard my dad's car.

"They're home!" Wily screamed.

"Act cool," I said, though I was shaking like a leaf.

"Get ready for a twenty-year time out," he groaned.

I saw the look in my Dad's eye. He was grumpy, he was tired. All he wanted to do was get inside and go to bed.

So I decided to be really cool and go out to greet them. "You're back so early."

My mother smiled. "I was worried that something had happened. So we came home right after dinner."

"What could have happened?" I smiled.

"Yeah," Wily said, "it was just another one of those quiet nights at home."

"That's good," my Dad said, quickly hugging us both. All he wanted to do was get ready for bed, which sounded good to me.

And that night, as I drifted off to sleep, I thought I felt the ghost of great-great-granddaddy Pinkerton sitting on my bed.

Nice job, Detective Patti Pinkerton, nice job, the ghost said, and then it faded away.

Coming from him, this detective felt pretty darn good about herself.

CHAPTER 25

Girl Detective

I had managed to solve my first case without my parents finding out. It wasn't that I lied. It was just that they didn't ask me about it.

The fact that they didn't know wasn't my fault and Wily certainly didn't want to tell them about his prank calls.

Neither Sarah nor Ramrod spilled the beans. They just winked and gave me the thumbs-up.

Since we weren't on speaking terms with the neighbors, no one told my parents about the bikers and the gators fighting around the house.

My sister came over the next afternoon and wanted to tell my folks all about what happened. It took every trick in the book to keep her quiet.

"But you solved the case," my sister said.

"That was just part of the job," I said modestly.

She looked at me and grinned. "You'll make a good policewoman one day."

"Detective," I said. "I want to be a detective."

"That's what you are now, Pink," she beamed.

"Hey, Patti," Ramrod shouted, "wanna hang ten?" My neighbor came blasting towards the house on his motorized skateboard.

I climbed aboard and sang *On the Road Again* off-key with Ramrod. Randy the gator bellowed as we rode by his cement gator wife. Susie Q just slept through it all and Pretty Girl the cat hissed from the roof of the house.

My mom watched us from the kitchen and my Dad sat arguing with the radio talk show in the living room. When I returned to my attic domain, I found a note pinned on my door from you-know-who:

You're the bravest girl I know.

That was a lot coming from my brother! I mean, how many monster brothers would care enough to write something like that?

Life was back to normal.

Except that now I was Patti "Pink" Pinkerton, detective. And there would be other cases to solve, other criminals to catch.

And we'll do it together.

Carla K. Tedrow

Carla K. Tedrow is an actress, author and book editor who manages to juggle her career with raising three young children in Florida. Born in Cape Girardeau, Missouri, Carla brings the values of her small town upbringing into her children's books, always striving to inspire and entertain.

Carla said, "Having read hundreds of books to my children over the years, I've developed a keen insight into what children want to hear and read. In each of my books I strive to capture their imagination, tickle their funnybones and leave them with a message."

Coming Soon
From FamilyVision Press™

PATTI PINKERTON #2

Beach Blanket Burglar

by Carla Tedrow

Everywhere Patti goes, adventure follows. This time, while vacationing with her family, she finds herself mixed up in another case. In this zany new mystery, Patti investigates the robberies at her hotel and finds herself face-to-face with the

BEACH BLANKET BURGLAR.